"Quinn, get down!"
"We're under fire!"

Bullets whizzed past Quinn's head and ricocheted off the rocks, sending debris and scrub raining down around them. There was nowhere to run, let alone hide.

The shots stopped. Quinn searched through the rain for their attacker and finally saw what they were facing. A remotely controlled drone was making a slow sweeping turn. Someone had jury-rigged it into a deadly weapon by welding a semiautomatic to the bottom.

Where was the person operating it? There was nothing around here for miles. And yet, in one terrifying moment of clarity, everything made sense.

And now it was coming back their way.

"Jeff!" she shouted. "What do we do?"

Maggie K. Black is an award-winning journalist and romantic suspense author with an insatiable love of traveling the world. She has lived in the American South, Europe and the Middle East. She now makes her home in Canada with her history-teacher husband, their two beautiful girls and a small but mighty dog. Maggie enjoys connecting with her readers at maggiekblack.com.

Visit the Author Profile page at LoveInspired.com for more titles.

SURVIVING THE WILDERNESS

MAGGIE K. BLACK

LOVE INSPIRED SUSPENSE

INSPIRATIONAL ROMANCE

LOVE INSPIRED® SUSPENSE
INSPIRATIONAL ROMANCE

Recycling programs for this product may not exist in your area.

ISBN-13: 978-1-335-55504-5

Surviving the Wilderness

Copyright © 2022 by Mags Storey

For questions and comments about the quality of this book, please contact us at CustomerService@Harlequin.com.

Love Inspired
22 Adelaide St. West, 41st Floor
Toronto, Ontario M5H 4E3, Canada
www.LoveInspired.com

Printed in U.S.A.

Then said Martha unto Jesus, Lord, if thou hadst been here, my brother had not died. But I know, that even now, whatsoever thou wilt ask of God, God will give it thee. Jesus saith unto her, Thy brother shall rise again.
—*John* 11:21-23

With thanks to Mike
for being such a relentless, determined and
unwavering advocate for our kids, and for all the ways you
stepped up and saved their lives that went unnoticed.

ONE

Water crashed down a sheer rock cliff just inches away from wilderness guide Quinn Dukes' feet with a force that was both majestic and deadly. At quarter after six in the morning in Northern Ontario, the predawn sun was still just a tiny sliver of gold against an otherwise pitch-black horizon. The waterfall she was about to descend in the darkness was at least five stories tall. The threat of impending rain felt heavy in the air. She tugged firmly on her belay rope, double-checked it was hooked securely to her climbing harness, and braced herself to leap backward. A light flickered in the trees far below to her right. She froze.

Had something gone wrong back at the campsite of the tour she was leading, and they'd sent someone looking for her?

A cold breeze brushed her skin. Today was the third and final day of her most challenging trip yet: leading over a dozen adults down a wild and raging river with the help of decently experienced co-guide named Bruno whom she'd been forced to hire at the last minute when her original pick had been struck and injured by a hit-

and-run driver. All the other tents had been silent, and her sister Rose had been only half awake when Quinn had slipped out of her sleeping bag.

Rose had been the one pushing her to take an hour to herself to pray and settle her mind before sunrise. Quinn had been surprised when Bruno had agreed to hold down the fort. Considering it would be about an hour before the sun fully rose and they weren't set to hit the rapids until nine, most of her campers would probably still be asleep by the time she got back.

It'd been a little over a year since Quinn had launched her very own wilderness adventure company. Ever since, she'd been caught between the joy of knowing she'd actually achieved her dream and the fear that she was just one wrong step away from losing it all. At just twenty-six, with the kind of long blond hair and freckles that made her look even younger, she knew some people didn't take her seriously and her fledgling company was still nowhere near breaking even. But a lot of her campers were incredibly active on social media and if they loved this adventure trip, the positive buzz could go a long way to keeping her dream alive.

Lord, I'm trying to trust You with my fears. Help me calm my heart.

She watched the figure move between the trees for a long moment, trying to determine if it was Rose or Bruno. But as whoever it was didn't seem to be in any particular hurry, she decided to rappel and meet them at the bottom.

Quinn wrapped the rope around her hand, leaped backward over the edge of the waterfall and felt her body free-fall for a single exhilarating moment. Then the toes of her boots touched the slippery rock again and she dug in hard. Adrenaline and happiness coursed through her. She leaped once more. Cold water tickled the side of her face. She belayed a few more feet to a thin, natural ledge then paused and looked around.

The person with the flashlight was a clearer shape now. He was a man, judging by his height and muscular appearance. A little over six feet tall, she thought, with strong arms and broad shoulders yet still looking like he could use a good meal. Several inches taller than Bruno and definitely not her sister. While many of the campers were physically fit, his distinctive build didn't quite match any of them. A shiver ran down her spine and through her arms into the fingers holding the rope.

Who was he? And what was he doing there?

The remote area was a spiderwebby maze of rivers hemmed in by towering rocks and thick trees. She hadn't seen so much as a roof shingle or tire track since they'd taken off from near Thunder Bay three days ago. The man switched off his flashlight and she stared at the darkness where his form had been just seconds ago. Then she continued down the waterfall, willing her nerves not to be rattled.

Truth be told, he did remind her of someone. Just not anyone she'd ever expected or wanted to see again. Despite how often he seemed to cross her mind.

Corporal Jefferey Connor of the Canadian Military Rangers was a complicated, reasonably handsome and incredibly moody man she'd worked with on similar trips for a large adventure company a couple of years back. At the time he'd just returned from serving his country overseas to work part-time for the branch of the military that saved lives inside Canada's borders. The tension in his jaw and sadness in his blue eyes had hinted he'd experienced something pretty bad on his last tour. Jeff had been fearless in the face of danger, incredible at leading trips and the most talented senior wilderness guide she'd ever worked under. But he'd been chronically incapable of asking anyone for help and had double-guessed every decision she'd made, treating her like a novice and pushing every single one of her buttons—including a few she hadn't even known she'd had.

They'd only worked together for four months, on both camping trips and teaching survival skills, before he disappeared suddenly for unspecified and mysterious "family reasons". And yet, for some unknown reason, the frustrating, infuriating man had been stuck in her mind like the fragment of some annoying song she couldn't stop humming ever since. This wouldn't be the first time she'd momentarily mistaken some total stranger for the one man she couldn't forget. Something told her it wouldn't be the last.

Quinn gritted her teeth and let her mind focus on the rush of the water beside her, the rope in her hands and the slippery rock beneath her feet.

There was a sudden yank on the rope, as if someone at the top of the falls was trying to shake her right off the side of the cliff.

"Hey!" she shouted. "Stop it! You could kill someone doing that!"

The rope shook again, this time succeeding in pulling her off the rock and sending her body swinging free. She looked up into the darkness, feeling fear and anger pound through her in equal measure as she tried to scramble for hand- and footholds.

"Who's up there?" she shouted. "This isn't funny! It's dangerous. Stop it right now!"

A flashlight clicked on above her. She gasped in confusion.

The face leering down at her was grotesque and rubbery, with small, beady eyes over a large hooked nose. The head was bald with wisps of hair sticking out over huge ears. It looked more troll-like than human. Her mind faltered as she tried to figure out what she was even seeing.

Then the rope gave way.

She fell in a helplessly tumbling free fall toward the water below.

Jeff ran through the forest so quickly he could barely feel his boots touch the ground. As a Canadian Ranger, rescuing those in danger and teaching people how to survive in the wilderness was what he was trained for. And as a man who'd witnessed far too many people die when he'd served his country overseas, the need to make sure the woman he'd just seen fall was okay pounded like a drum through his core.

The waterfall—a daring, gutsy, dangerous climb— lay on just one of many winding branches springing from the large and fast river that cut through towering, sheer-granite rock near his cabin. The water in the spring-fed pool at the base was shockingly cold and would be enough to knock the breath from even the strongest swimmer's lungs.

He'd tackled the waterfall himself a couple of times

since he and his little girl had moved to the rustic and remote former hunter's cabin. When Jeff suddenly learned he had a child, he'd had to get the toddler as far away as possible from the angry man who'd been cruelly led to believe he was her real father before the death of her mother, Della, had led to the truth coming out.

Jeff and Della had a very brief and unhappy relationship while serving together overseas. He'd had no idea Della was pregnant with his daughter Addison when she'd abruptly ended it. Paul had then started dating Della, and they'd been engaged to marry when she'd died.

Addison had been living with her grandmother while both Paul and Della served in separate units overseas, but still Jeff couldn't imagine the pain Paul had felt when he'd been told not only was his fiancée dead, but a DNA test had proved Addison was another man's child.

Since then Paul had started posting things online in the dark edges of the web questioning just how Jeff had managed to survive the makeshift drone attack that had killed her and thirteen other soldiers serving in Jeff and Della's military unit.

When his older brother Vic, who was staying with him and Addison for a while, had told Jeff that a dozen campers had pulled their canoes ashore in a narrow cove that sliced a jagged gap in the rock face, and hiked up into the woods to set up tents, Jeff had been more shocked than irritated. His nearest town was over an hour's drive away. The cabin was so deep into the wilderness, it was completely off the grid, leaving them to rely on a well for water, generators for electricity and wood-burning stoves for heat.

But now, as his eyes trained on the deep pool at the base of the falls, watching the water beat relentlessly against branches and logs, pushing them down into its depths, he knew there was something far worse than seeing some a stranger saunter onto his land—knowing he'd let her die there. Jeff's first-aid training was pretty extensive, and Vic had served as a military medic before coming home to be with his late wife as she'd died of cancer. The climber just needed to survive until he could reach her. He pushed himself faster, until his chest ached like it was on fire and his throat felt scorched with smoke.

"God, I've seen way too many people die. I can't bear to lose anyone else. Help me to save her before it's too late."

The prayer slipped through Jeff's lips in a hoarse rasp before he'd even realized it. No, he didn't pray anymore. Let alone ask God—or anyone else—for help. Not since the roadside drone attack two years ago that had taken out so many of his unit. He should've been there, driving the convoy to the remote outpost from base. If he had been, maybe he'd have seen the drone and warned those behind him. Or taken it down himself and saved their lives.

Instead he'd been sitting in the brig for telling off a superior officer he'd thought was mistreating the newer recruits. The closest he'd come to crying out to God had been months later, standing in the back of the church during Della's memorial service, after her mother had told him the little girl with luminous blue eyes and long blond curls who she'd been raising was secretly his.

And that urge to pray for God's help had been swallowed up in anger.

He broke through the trees and saw the climber. She was lying limp on her back in the water. Long blond hair streamed over her face and floated in the water around her shoulders. He couldn't tell if she was breathing.

"Hang on!" he shouted. "I'm coming to get you."

He yanked off his jacket and tossed it on the rocks, but didn't pause long enough to unlace his boots. Jeff dove in, surfaced and gasped a breath as the unexpected cold hit his system. Water soaked his clothes, threatening to drag him down. The roar of the falls was deafening. He ignored both, focused only on her.

In two strokes, he was by her side. He slid his right arm beneath her shoulders, pulled her to him and carefully swam her to shore. She gasped a breath and sudden hope filled his heart. He climbed the slippery rocks and pulled her up alongside him. The belay rope was still attached to her harness and he dragged it onto the shore. Then he sat there, on the ground, his legs folded beneath him and the woman in his arms. Her chest rose and fell as her breaths stuttered. His hands gently brushed the side of her neck and he felt her fluttering weak pulse beneath his fingertips. So far, so good. Then, for the first time, he really looked into the eyes of the woman he'd rescued. His heart stopped.

"Quinn?" he asked. "Quinn Dukes?"

Was it really her? The most beautiful, gutsy and infuriating woman he'd ever met was lying limp in his arms and barely breathing.

She jolted and sat up so quickly their foreheads collided. He winced as pain shot through his skull.

"Jeff?" Her eyes snapped open. Confusion filled their dark brown depths. "Is it really you?"

"What are you doing here?" he asked. "How did you find me?"

"Find you?" she asked. "I wasn't looking for you." She glanced to his arms encircling her body then back to his face just inches from hers. Her eyes widened. "Why…why are you hugging me?"

Hugging? Jeff was so flabbergasted, he'd have leaped up if that hadn't meant dropping her.

"You fell into the water and I pulled you out!" he practically spluttered. "Don't you remember?"

"No, not really," she said slowly. "I remember seeing you in the woods, someone yanking the rope, and looking up to see what looked like a troll." She struggled to straighten in his arms. A weak smile crossed her lips. "Although I do remember that Jeff Connor avoids touching people unless their life is actually on the line."

What did that mean? When they'd worked together, Quinn had been an endless beacon of cheeriness who'd never hesitated to throw an arm around a camper in need and dolled out high fives and fist bumps in every direction. But she was the weird one, not him. She'd also been incessantly positive and never stopped asking questions.

"Are you hurt?" he asked.

"I feel like a did a swan dive into a concrete floor," Quinn said. "But I don't think anything's broken or sprained."

"And you think you saw a troll face?"

Her eyes darted to the top of the waterfall. He followed her gaze, but there was nothing there.

Fear prickled at the back of his neck. Had Paul finally found his home? Was he coming for Addison?

Quinn closed her eyes for a long moment and he watched her lips move in what looked like a silent prayer.

A siren rose and fell faintly in the distance.

Quinn's eyes widened. "What's that?" she asked.

"My security alarm," Jeff said. One he'd installed in every cabin window in case Paul ever made good on his threats. "Someone's trying to break into my cabin."

TWO

The alarm stopped just as abruptly as it had started, which, he was positive, meant his brother was there and had entered the code. But Jeff still felt the color drain from his face.

When he'd installed a security system in a cabin so remote it didn't even have a phone line, his brother had told him bluntly but gently that he'd thought Paul was just a harmless man in pain who was lashing out in grief. He reminded him that, despite his angry rhetoric, Paul hadn't even gone to Della's memorial service or tried to fight it through the courts when Addison's grandmother gave Jeff custody. Vic had added the fact that Jeff was always on edge. That his flinching at every car backfire, siren wail and whiff of acrid smoke had more to do with Jeff's own powerfully painful memories of standing under the hot sun in a distant country, staring at the charred remains of an attack that should've taken his life.

If he was honest, sometimes Jeff almost suspected he was right. Before an intruder had actually tripped the security alarm.

"I thought nobody lived up here," Quinn said. "There's nothing on the map for miles."

Yeah, and he liked it that way.

"How do you know it's not just a squirrel or raccoon?" Quinn added.

"Because wild animals don't mess with high-security keypads." He eased her from his arms and stood. Then reached out a hand and helped her up. "I live in an old hunting cabin not far from here, with my older brother. Vic's a former military medic."

"I remember you telling me about him," she said. "His wife has cancer, right?"

"She passed away last year," Jeff said.

"I'm so sorry."

I also live with my daughter Addison. She's three, and I never told you about her back when we were working together because that was before I even knew I had a kid. That's why I quit without explanation. Because suddenly I had custody of this little toddler I never even knew was mine. Her mother had told everyone that Addison was another man's daughter and I only found out the truth at her memorial service.

The words crossed his mind but somehow froze before they reached his lips. He wasn't ready to have that conversation with anyone yet. Especially her.

"I'm sorry, I guess one of the campers came looking for me," Quinn said.

"By trying to climb in a window?"

She didn't answer. Instead she fiddled with the rope on her harness, but her limbs were shaking.

"Let me," he said. He leaned over, unclipped the

rope from the harness and slung it across his shoulder. "Now, I'm going to carry you."

"No, you won't—"

"Quinn," he said so firmly she blinked. "Imagine you've got a camper who's just fallen some thirty feet backward off a waterfall and is at risk of a concussion. Would you let them walk off a fall like that, when it's still not light out and they're in a completely unknown location?"

He'd never heard that tone of voice come out of his own mouth before. It was similar to the protective and caring way he talked to his daughter, only coming from a much different, deeper and more equal place. He wasn't sure what to make of it.

"Fine." Quinn reached her arms around his neck. "Just don't drop me."

He chuckled despite himself, swept her up into his arms, and ran through the trees. He could feel her shaking even harder now as her initial adrenaline burst wore off. Moments later, the cabin came into view. It was a two-story structure made of logs thicker than a man's torso. The wilds of Canada were dotted with such buildings, built over a hundred years ago, from when the river was the major mode of transport for the lumber and fur trades. But most had been abandoned or deserted long ago. He spotted Vic standing outside the main door as he approached. Even at a distance, he could see his brother's eyebrows rise at the sight of a woman in Jeff's arms.

"What happened?" Jeff yelled.

"Don't know," Vic shouted back. "Laundry room window alarm went haywire. I turned it off and checked the interior of the house. It was clean. Addison's still asleep, so I was waiting on you before I did a perimeter search so that she wouldn't be alone."

"Got it!" Jeff bellowed.

"Who's Addison?" Quinn asked.

"We got company?" Vic shouted.

He opened his mouth but couldn't figure out where to start with either question. So, instead, he just ran past his red pickup and Vic's black one to the front door and pushed inside.

The main floor was divided into a living room and kitchen. A narrow staircase of split logs led upstairs to the second floor. Jeff dropped the belay rope by the front door. Then he set Quinn down on an oversize couch and draped a heavy quilt over her. A battery-operated video monitor on the table flickered gently with the small black-and-white image of his daughter sleeping.

"Who's Addison?" Quinn asked again.

"She is." Jeff gestured the screen, waiting for her to ask the next question and then the next as he tiptoed toward a truth he didn't want to tell her one word at a time.

Instead, all Quinn said was, "She's sweet. I'm guessing you and Vic are raising her here after her mom died?"

"Yeah," he said. And that's when he realized she'd assumed Addison was Vic's daughter. He had to tell her the truth and he would. Just as soon as he found the right words. He turned away from her, toward the fire already burning in the hearth, knelt and added a couple of extra logs.

"How do you have electricity up here?" she asked.

Quinn's eyes were on his face, somehow even larger and more luminous than he remembered. "I have multiple generators and use a lot of batteries—"

"And you're running a security system?"

"I go through a lot of gas," he admitted. "Now, I'm not Vic, but is it okay if I check you for injuries? Just the standard first-aid thing."

"Go ahead," she said, "my body feels like it's all pins and needles, but I'm sure nothing's broken."

He sat by her feet on the couch, helped her out of her boots, and then gently ran his hands over her feet, getting her to press her soles against his palms, checking to see if her legs were sprained or broken. Then he leaned forward and wordlessly reached for her hands. She slid her fingers into his and he repeated the same test to test how hard she could push against him. Then, her hands lingered in his.

"You're right," he said. "Nothing seems broken."

The door swung open and his brother filled the doorway. Jeff jumped to his feet. With the same brown hair, blue eyes and tall stature, Vic and Jeff were often mistaken for each other when apart, especially when they'd both been in the military.

But side by side, the differences were obvious. Vic was half an inch shorter, his shoulders about three inches wider, his beard thick where Jeff barely had more than stubble. Vic's eyes were grayish blue where Jeff's had hints of green. Not to mention their military careers had taken very different paths and Vic had fallen for woman who'd been a loving, devoted wife and friend to him until the day she'd died.

"Whoever tried to jimmy the window has taken off

without a trace," Vic said and kicked off his boots. "I'd call the police but it'll take them a couple of hours to get here and considering it's supposed to rain all day I'm not expecting they'll find much of anything."

"Agreed." Jeff nodded.

"I'm guessing she's one of the campers, and she was injured in the woods?" Vic asked.

"Yup. Quinn Dukes—" Quinn stuck out her hand "—I'm guessing you're Vic?"

"Guilty as charged." Vic strode across the room and shook her hand gently. "You the same Quinn Dukes who worked with Jeff a couple of years back?"

Quinn nodded. "Probably."

Jeff's heart stopped. What had he told his brother about her? That she was infuriating? Irritating? Impressive? Breathtaking? Probably all of the above?

"I take it you had an accident?" Vic asked, his countenance switching from older brother to medic in an instant. "Are you hurt?"

"I was belaying and fell down a waterfall," Quinn said. "And I'm fine."

"She fell at least thirty feet, which could've killed her," Jeff said. "And she thinks she saw someone who might've intentionally caused her to fall. I reckon she was in the water for less than five minutes before I got her out, and she doesn't have any obvious injuries. But she was dazed."

"Any confusion?" Vic queried.

"I thought I saw a rubbery troll face," Quinn said.

"Any history of head trauma?"

"Well, I used to climb in and out of my second-floor bedroom window as a teenager," Quinn said. "Once, I fell so hard, I sprained my ankle, conked my head and thought I saw sky sharks circling above me."

She laughed at the memory, but Vic's face was serious.

"I'm going to check you for a concussion before we take you back to camp," Vic said. "Although the troll you saw might've been a perfectly normal person or even a rock. Adrenaline and trauma do crazy things to the brain chemistry." His eyes met Jeff's pointedly. "Sometimes they linger for years if they're not addressed."

The last thing Jeff needed right now was another brotherly lecture about getting trauma counseling or finding God. Someone had actually tried to break into their home. Clearly, the fear of danger he was unable to shake wasn't all in his mind.

He excused himself and went upstairs to change into clean and dry clothes. His heart was thumping like he'd just run a marathon. Quinn had looked so strong and confident leaping down the falls. Someone like her didn't just fall without a reason. Had somebody actually tried to kill her? And what did that have to do with a person trying to break into his house?

He stood for a long moment outside his daughter's room, eased the door open a crack and listened to the soft sound of her breaths rising and falling, along with the gentle high-pitched wheeze of her golden retriever puppy, Butterscotch. Despite Jeff's best efforts to convince them that sleeping dogs belonged on the floor, the little yellow ball of fur was curled up tightly beside his daughter on the bed, wedged between her and a giant golden-haired ragdoll almost as big as Addison herself.

He felt a sad smile cross his lips as he started down the stairs. Everything about the way Addison had come into the world felt wrong. It had started with an inappropriate relationship between him and a fellow soldier named Della in his unit. When he'd tried to take the relationship public and make it on the level, she had refused and broken it off, saying Jeff wasn't cut out to be anyone's husband or father. Then she started a relationship with another man, gotten engaged to him before Addison was born and listed her then fiancé, Paul, on Addison's birth certificate.

It had been Della's own mother who'd told him the truth and gotten the DNA test to prove it. She'd urged him to forgive Della and told him that Della's estranged father, also former military, had been so controlling and abusive, they'd had a restraining order against him, moved constantly and even changed their names. "People who've been hurt sometimes let that hurt make them toxic," she'd told him, "which is why it's important to try and forgive."

Funny thing was, forgiving Della was the easy part. The person he couldn't forgive was himself.

His brother met him at the foot of the stairs.

"All good news," Vic said. "No major injuries or signs of concussion. She'll be sore for a while. But she knew how to fall safely, and God was looking out for her."

Jeff resisted the urge to point out that his brother sure gave God a lot of credit for a man who'd seen his wife—the love of Vic's life—die of cancer in her twenties. Vic meant well, he always did, and though he'd never admitted it, Jeff almost admired how his brother had his faith to fall back on.

Jeff found Quinn curled up on the couch where he'd left her, now dressed in his own gray track suit that he'd left in the dryer. Her damp blond hair fell loose around her shoulders. Large and dark eyes scanned his face.

His mouth went dry. How could she possibly be more beautiful than he remembered?

"I hope it's okay if I borrow this while my clothes are in the dryer," she said. "I promise I'll be out of your hair soon and back on the river."

"I don't really like the idea of you paddling off with someone out there who might've caused your accident or tried to break into my house," he said and sat on the arm of the couch.

"Yeah, I get that," she said. "But there's no reason to suspect any of my campers. Besides, our end destination is only four hours by canoe but over eight in the car—even if we did have enough vehicles here to transport fifteen people, which we don't.

"I've got everyone's luggage and electronic devices waiting for them when we get there, not to mention there's a regional police station where I can walk in and report everything that's happened. And even if someone in my group messed with my rope and tried to break into your cabin—which I can't imagine unless it was someone's idea of a misguided prank—they're not going to try something in a convoy of canoes."

She smiled, but he didn't.

"If there's someone dangerous lurking in the woods," Quinn said, "there's no reason to believe it has anything to do with me."

"So, it's a coincidence this happened when you were there?" he asked.

"The details of this trip were all over social media," she said. "People actually voted on what route they wanted to take. So, for all we know, somebody was after you and used my group as cover."

He shuddered involuntarily, as if someone had just poured something clammy down the back of his shirt. She leaned forward, took his hand and squeezed it reassuringly. Their fingers linked and there was something both soft and strong about her touch. Then he pulled away.

"There's no home phone or cell phone signal up here," he said. "But did Vic give you the satellite phone to contact the camp?"

"He did," she said. "I got through to my sister Rose. She's said she'd go wake up Bruno and let him know we might be leaving a little late."

"Bruno Jones?" Jeff asked. He grimaced. He'd worked with Bruno before. The man was a talented enough guide, despite the fact he'd racked up gambling debt and owed a lot of people money. Not to mention, Jeff had caught him trying to sneak a flask of vodka onto more than one trip. "I can't believe you'd work for that clown."

"I'm not," Quinn said, stiffly. "It's my company, and he works for me. Wasn't my first choice for this trip, but the guide I'd initially hired was in a car crash last week and Bruce stepped in at the last minute."

Jeff opened his mouth and found no words coming out. When they'd worked together, she'd talked incessantly about wanting to run her own wilderness adventure company. Here, she'd actually gone and gone it.

"I'm sorry," he said. "I feel like an idiot. Let me start again. So, you have your own business?"

"I do." She smiled. "I was just spinning my wheels at the old place. I kept applying for promotions and not getting them. Apparently, there was some weird rumor going around that I was difficult to work with and that some senior guide had refused to work with me or have me on his trips?"

His breath caught. Had that been him?

Quinn's eyes rolled at the memory.

"So I struck out on my own," she went on. "Now I'm my own boss and run the whole shebang."

He whistled softly, feeling a lot of admiration and a little pang of jealousy.

"I've got twelve campers on this trip, ranging in age between barely twenty and mid-sixties," she went on. "It's three days of paddling and four nights of camping, ending tonight."

"And people voted for this trip online?" he asked.

"Yup," she said. "I find it gets people excited about the trip when they feel like they had a part in putting it together." She shifted her legs under her and instinctively he slid off the arm of the couch and sat beside her. "One of my loyal campers named Marcel is a podcaster and computer programmer. He's absolutely addicted to cartography. He's always sending me maps of out-of-the-way places."

The joy that radiated through her was so palpable, it was like he could reach out and touch it. He'd forgotten what it was like to be around Quinn and the

sheer amount of enthusiasm and optimism she brought
to every moment of life. Everything had seemed so
harsh, serious, and hard when he'd returned from overseas, gotten a job as a wilderness guide, enlisted for
parttime service with the Rangers and started life anew
in Canada. And there she'd been with her long blond
hair, freckled nose and infectious grin, looking more
like some pretty starlet than someone who had any idea
of what roughing it was actually like.

They'd worked together for a few months, including
navigating several trips together. She'd been a junior
wilderness guide. He'd been the senior one, who'd led
the instructional activities back at the main camp as
well as hiking expeditions, canoeing and camping trips.

She'd asked questions constantly, as though every
second was an opportunity to learn something new.
But she'd been confident too and quick to tell him when
she thought he was wrong. He'd felt like a man stuck in
the darkness, and everything about her had seemed too
alive and too bright. It was like the fledgling attractions
he'd felt for other women in the past but cranked up to
a million. So he'd pushed her away emotionally and, as
the senior guide on their trips, had made her life harder
than it needed to be.

When he'd been called into their boss's office to
learn that the two of them had been chosen to lead a
prestigious, isolated expedition at the very northern
edges of the province, something inside him had almost panicked at the thought of working so closely in
such a remote place.

Heat rose to the back of his neck.

"Well, for what it's worth, I'm sorry for being so

hard on you when we worked together," he said. "I had a pretty big chip on my shoulder back then, which had nothing to do with you. But I know I told people, including our boss, that I didn't like working with you and didn't want you on any more trips that I lead. But only because there was this weird tension between us and I was worried about us working too closely together—"

His feeble attempt at an explanation froze on his tongue as Quin's eyes snapped to his face. She swung her feet around to the floor and stood.

"Hang on, you're the one who went around bad-mouthing me?" she said. "All this time I've been fighting to achieve my dreams and it turns out you were the one who sabotaged me?"

Quinn hadn't stopped to check her limbs were steady before leaping to her feet, but now that she was standing, she was pleasantly surprised at how strong she felt. Jeff was a good six inches taller than she was and she couldn't really remember actually having looked down at him before. But now, as he sat there with his mouth hanging open and his blue eyes wide, she almost felt sorry for raising her voice. Almost, but not quite, considering Jeff might be the skunk who'd tried to tank her reputation.

"I'm sorry," Jeff said. "But they were planning on sending the two of us alone up north to lead a very challenging trip and I was afraid the tensions between us added an unnecessary risk."

What tensions between them? She was a hundred percent certain Jeff had had no clue about the fledgling crush she'd had on him. And she'd never been anything but a very capable professional.

"There were no tensions between us." She waved at the space in between them for emphasis. Then circled her hand in the air as if painting an invisible circle around his face. "All the tension was radiating off you."

"Okay." He raised a hand palm up as if to deflect her words. "I'll admit I was pretty grouchy back then and—"

"Grouchy?" she repeated. "Do you have any idea how downright intimidating it was for me to work with you? You were older, taller, physically stronger, and you'd served our country overseas. You seemed indestructible. I wanted to be a team. But it was like you were doggedly determined not to accept my help with anything. Instead you seemed devoted to criticizing every single thing I did, and never once gave me the benefit of the doubt."

The words hung between them for a moment and she almost expected him to backtrack.

Instead he crossed his arms. "Maybe. To be completely honest, you're not the first person to tell me I'm incapable of accepting help."

He held her gaze for a long moment and somehow neither of them looked away. She felt something twist inside her chest.

"But sometimes it's better to do things yourself than risk letting someone else put lives in danger," he added. "And right now, all that matters is making sure we get to the bottom of everything that's happened today. So, I'd like to drive you back to your camp and talk to your campers to see if they know anything about either the prowler or your accident."

Like she wanted him anywhere near her campsite and campers after what he'd just admitted.

She closed her eyes and prayed. *Lord, I need Your wisdom and Your grace, because right now all I feel is frustrated, worried and angry.*

"Coffee's ready!" Vic called. She opened her eyes. Jeff's brother was standing in the kitchen doorway. "What do you take in yours, Quinn?"

"Milk, please," Quinn said. "Maple syrup too if you have it."

Vic's grin widened. "Amber or dark?"

"Dark," Quinn said. "Thanks."

"No problem," Vic said. "Your boots have gotta be soaked, but I have a pair of my wife's old ones you can wear until they dry."

"Thank you," she said again. "Jeff told me about her. I'm really sorry for your loss."

His smile both deepened and grew sadder.

"Thank you," Vic said. "It'll be a year next month. We had ten years together as best friends—eight of them as husband and wife. I'd rather have had that time with her than a whole lifetime with anyone else."

A lump formed in Quinn's throat and before she could clear it enough to speak, Vic disappeared into the kitchen, leaving her alone again. She wondered what it was like to love someone like that.

A buzzer went off. It sounded like a large and angry mosquito trapped in a metal box.

"That'll be the dryer," Jeff said. He stood awkwardly and shifted his weight from one foot to another. "Sometimes it needs an extra few minutes. I'll be back in a moment."

He disappeared through the doorway. Quinn walked over to the rope on the floor, crouched and slowly ran it between her fingers. There didn't seem to be anything wrong with it. No knicks, cuts or signs of foul play.

She closed her eyes again and prayed. *Help me see what I need to see.*

The rope tugged out of her hands as Quinn heard a fierce but tiny growl. She peaked around the corner. A golden retriever puppy, of no more than five months old, was playfully nipping at her climbing rope. She smiled slightly and flicked it. The dog jumped back, barked and wagged its tail, as if expecting the rope to bite him back. Quinn giggled.

"Tha' my dog," a small voice said proudly from behind her.

Quinn turned. A little girl, about three years old, was standing behind her in yellow pajamas with butterflies on them. Golden hair trailed in long, loose curls down her back.

"Hi," she said. "My name's Quinn. With a Q. You must be Addison."

"Hello." Bright blue eyes regarded her seriously.

"You have a very good dog," Quinn said.

"No!" the girl said brightly. "Bu'er'scotch is naugh'y dog."

"A naughty dog?" Quinn asked. Butterscotch was now rolling on his back, underneath the rope, apparently having lost his imaginary battle.

"Yes." She nodded vigorously. "He's a t'ief!"

"A thief?" Quinn asked, widening her eyes.

"Uh-huh." The girl threw her arms around the puppy. Butterscotch dropped the rope, and licked her on the nose. "He steal Daddy socks!"

Quinn tossed her head back and laughed. She sat cross-legged beside them on the floor.

Addison scooted over to Quinn and the dog commando-crawled after her. "You got a dog?"

"No," Quinn said, "but my big sister Leia has a cat named Moses."

The little girl tilted her head to the side as if trying to figure out whether a cat was worth talking about. Then her smile widened. "I saw a bunny!"

"You did?" Quinn asked. "Where?"

"Ou'side!"

Quinn leaned on her elbows, feeling the fire warm her back and listened as the little girl launched into a long and enthusiastic story about a rabbit she'd seen in the woods. Something in Quinn's heart ached for her. She hadn't been much older when her own mother had died and, like her, she'd grown up in the remote Canadian wilderness. Only, she'd had two older sisters and one younger one, and while her father had been suspicious of the outside world, they hadn't been that far from the closest town.

Quinn prayed God would surround Addison with happiness, love, and people who'd be family to her.

A footstep creaked the floor. She looked over. Vic was back with a red travel mug.

"I see you've met Addison," he said.

"I did," Quinn said. "She was telling me about how Butterscotch steals your socks."

"Not my socks," Vic said with a grin. "The little

brat only goes after Jeff's." He set the coffee down and looked at Addison. "Isn't that right, Sunshine?"

The little girl nodded, sending her curls flying. "Bu'er'scotch only eat Daddy socks! Uncle Vic socks too yucky!"

Quinn rose slowly. This little bundle of happiness was Jeff's daughter?

Jeff was a father and he'd never told her?

THREE

Even slightly damp, Quinn's sweatshirt still smelled like her. Jeff held it to his chest for a long moment, as if it were a life jacket that would keep his sinking heart from drowning. Then he tossed it back in the dryer, set the timer for another few minutes, and waited while it spun. When he finally gathered up her clothes and walked into the kitchen, Vic was standing by the sink.

"I have to leave shortly for a meeting with my commanding officer about my next deployment," Vic said. "He's up in this area from Ottawa and we agreed to meet in Kilpatrick." Jeff nodded and kept walking through the kitchen. "As you know, I've decided to enter the Canadian Armed Forces' training program to become an emergency medical surgeon. I start in five weeks."

Jeff stopped and turned around. "Could we talk about that later?"

"We could," Vic said. "Unless you're just going to keep avoiding having a real conversation until after I pack my bags and leave."

Jeff winced. Vic took a slow sip of his coffee.

"I don't like the idea of leaving you here all alone

with Addison when I go on deployment," Vic went on, "especially after what happened today. I know you had a bad experience with that day care you tried enrolling her in. But you need to think through what's going to happen when she starts school and who's going to take care of her when you're on deployment."

The day care program had been in a small town over an hour away, and he'd only enrolled Addison because Vic had encouraged him, telling him that Addison needed to socialize with kids her own age. Jeff was pretty sure Vic had also been secretly hoping he'd use the time to meet people, make friends, get involved in a church, sports team or club, and maybe even get that grief counseling he kept pushing for.

Addison had loved it.

But something about her favorite teacher, Kelsey, had rubbed Jeff the wrong way. Kelsey's father had served in the military and, sadly, had died of a heart attack a few years back while on his daily jog around the base. So now she and her deadbeat brother were living with their uncle—who also happened to be Vic's pastor. She'd seemed all together too interested in Addison and getting close to his little girl.

Jeff blew out a hard breath and realized he'd hugged the laundry closer. Unless a major emergency hit the country and he was called up for service, he wasn't scheduled to be deployed for a few months yet. He'd have something figured out by then.

"I appreciate you looking out for me," Jeff said. "But in case you missed it, there's a bunch of way more important stuff going on all around us today. Your timing for all this couldn't be worse."

Plus, he'd already gotten one indictment on his stubbornness and inability to accept help today. He hardly needed another one.

"You've hidden yourself away from the world for over a year," Vic said, "and now someone you used to work with has just randomly showed up on your doorstep. Maybe she's here for a reason. Even if it's just for you to finally have a chat with someone who isn't your brother."

That would mean knowing how to even start the conversation. Jeff turned and started for the living room, only to then stop dead in the doorway as he caught sight of the scene unfolding in front of him. Quinn sat cross-legged on the floor with Butterscotch curled up beside her on one side and his daughter Addison on the other. Addison had leaned her head against Quinn's shoulder. Their voices rose and, like music, Addison's happy chattering formed the melody and Quinn's caring responses the harmony. Then Quinn looked up and met his eyes, and his chest grew even tighter.

"Daddy!" Addison leaped to her feet and ran over to Jeff. "I have a new friend!"

She pointed dramatically at Quinn.

"I see." Jeff dropped Quinn's clothes on the couch, swept his daughter up into his arms and held her close.

"Your daughter is absolutely amazing," Quinn said. "We've been having a wonderful time." The sweetness of Quinn's voice didn't keep him from noticing the questions in her eyes. "I didn't know you had a child."

"It's not something I find easy to talk about," Jeff admitted.

"I got your clothes," he added, nodding to the obvious pile he'd just deposited in front of her. "I'll take Addison to get changed then, when you're ready, we can get you back to camp."

"Come too?" Addison asked hopefully.

"Absolutely," he said.

"Bu'er'scotch come too?"

"Sure," he agreed. He was already planning to drop by the top of the waterfall on the way, and the puppy could use a walk.

"Giant Dolly too?" Addison pressed.

"No." He laughed and turned to Quinn. "Giant Dolly is a two-and-a-half-foot-tall rag doll that's almost the same size she is. Addison can't sleep without her." He looked back at his daughter. "But you can bring your pink-and-blue puppy backpack and your walkie-talkie, okay?"

Addison's brows knit, as if debating whether this was a reasonable comprise, before she nodded. He took her upstairs to get dressed and came back to find Quinn dressed in her own clothes and Vic's wife's hiking boots.

They walked first to the waterfall with Addison on his shoulders but didn't find so much as a suspicious rock or twig out of place.

Then they drove to the campgrounds, through a combination of winding dirt tracks and off-road driving, until he saw the peaks of tents rising through the trees. He rolled down the window and smelled the aroma of sizzling bacon and eggs. Before he'd even stopped the truck, he saw a blond woman running toward them. She was a couple of inches shorter than Quinn and her build was curvy where Quinn's was lithe, but even in a glance it was unmistakable she and Quinn were sisters.

"Hey, thanks for helping hold down the fort," Quinn called and leaped out the door. "Jeff, this is my little sister Rose. Rose, this is Jeff."

"You're with the Canadian Rangers, right?" Rose asked.

"Yes, ma'am."

Rose glanced to the sky and whispered, "Thank You, Lord," and Jeff realized that she was thanking God for him.

Rose turned to Quinn and he saw the waves of worry filling her eyes. "We've got a problem. Bruno's missing."

"What do you mean he's missing?" Quinn felt her voice rise. She ran around to the other side of the vehicle to join her sister. "Last I saw him, it was about ten at night. He was by the fire. I reminded him that I'd be going for a climb first thing in the morning but would be back by breakfast. He said, 'Good for you,' clapped me on the back and wished me good-night. Then he went into his tent."

"I just assumed he was still sleeping in until I just checked his tent and found him gone," Rose said. "I've asked around and nobody's seen him since last night."

Jeff got out of the truck. "I take it he wasn't sharing a tent with anyone?" he asked.

"No," Quinn said. "He was the odd man out and everyone else had a tent buddy. I was sharing with Rose."

"What's the current mood at the camp like?" Jeff asked.

"A bit tense," Rose said, "but not too tense."

"Anyone seem too calm and relaxed?" he prompted.

She crinkled her nose. "I don't know. People are still waking up and most just seem sleepy."

Jeff opened the back door and lifted Addison out of her car seat. The puppy half leaped and half tumbled out onto the ground after her. He set his daughter down and helped her put on a small backpack covered with pink and blue dogs Quinn vaguely knew were on a popular children's television show.

"And are all other campers accounted for?" Quinn asked.

"Yup," Rose said. "When I realized Bruno was missing, I did a complete head count."

"Thank you," Quinn said.

"No problem." Rose crouched down to Addison's eye level and stuck out her hand. "Hi, my name's Rose and I'm Quinn's little sister."

Quinn's eyes met Jeff's and she was able to read the tempest of questions brewing in their blue depths before he even asked.

"Is it possible that Bruno caused your fall and tried to break into my house?" Jeff asked.

"Practically speaking, yes it's possible," she said. "He definitely had enough time and the physical ability to yank my rope free and then run to your cabin. But I can't believe he would either break into your home or risk my life like that."

"You know he drinks sometimes," Jeff said.

"Yeah, and I can totally see him sneaking off for a predawn sip of vodka from that flask of his and falling in the river. But not this."

She felt Addison's small hand take hers and squeeze. She looked down to see the girl looking up at her. "I hungry."

"I did actually try to get her to eat something before we left," Jeff said apologetically. "But she never likes to eat until she's been up awhile."

"Well, it's a good thing Rose has got eggs, toast and sausage cooking," Quinn said brightly.

Addison glanced at Rose. "Dogs like sausage."

Rose laughed. "Well then, let's all go get some."

She stretched out her hand to Addison, who took it without letting go of Quinn's on her other side. Then they walked toward the tents, Jeff beside Quinn and Butterscotch trailing after them.

Rock towered high and sheer on both sides of the river, creating a deep channel of rapidly flowing water. But there was a small and sandy cove nestled between two jutting cliffs, where Quinn's group had grounded their canoes before hiking up into a clearing in the trees to pitch their tents.

People clustered in ones and twos between the tents and fire pit. Several waved and called "good morning" in her direction. She smiled and called back greetings in response. But no one seemed in a hurry to saunter her way. Then again, the sun had barely risen less than an hour ago. The smell of campfire coffee and food mingled with the scent of damp earth and pine trees. Rose led Addison away to folding tables where a small portable grill sizzled. The little girl waved a small pink plastic clamshell at Jeff. He pulled a matching one from his pocket and waved it back.

"What are those?" Quinn asked.

"Walkie-talkies," Jeff said. "Addison absolutely loves them and they've got an incredibly impressive range. That's her way of reminding me she can call me if she needs to."

He scanned her campers. There was something so intense about his gaze, she wondered what he was looking for.

"The muscular man sitting by the fire with the shaved head…" he said after a long moment. "Is he law enforcement?"

"Don?" she said. "No, he's private security. Why?"

"The way he looked me over makes me think not much gets past him," Jeff said. "He might've seen something. Also, the thin woman clutching her tin mug…"

"Suzanne," she supplied.

"She's addicted to nicotine and itching for a cigarette," Jeff said. "She might've snuck out at night for one. Any idea what the tall woman by the fire is scribbling in that notebook?"

"Charis is an author," she said. "Self-published with a huge online following. Writes about this incredible handsome detective who does karate and solves crime."

"Huh." It was amazing how loaded a single syllable could be. Then he smiled. "Guessing you wish he was here with you now instead of me?"

She felt a smile turn on her lips.

"Hey, Jeff?" A man who looked to be in his sixties, judging by the lines etched in his sun-tanned face, shoulder-length gray hair and long beard rushed across the ground toward him. "Long time! How you been, man?"

She watched as Jeff's shoulders stiffened.

"Who is he and how does he know who I am?" Jeff asked hurriedly under his breath. "He's vaguely familiar but normally I never forget a face."

"Kirk used to take trips with us through our old job," she said. "He was on at least one that we led together. Former Canadian military."

"Air force." Kirk reached out with a suntanned arm and shook Jeff's hand.

"Good to see you," Jeff said.

"Didn't know if you'd recognize me," Kirk said with a chuckle. "I was clean-shaven with a buzz cut last time you saw me. Then I figured if I was now retired, I might as well look it."

A sudden crash sounded, followed by Addison shouting, "Naugh'y dog! No t'ief!"

They looked over to see Butterscotch wagging his tail at an overturned plastic plate with what looked like the remains of someone's abandoned meal scattered on the ground.

"Well, that's what someone gets for leaving their plate unattended," Quinn said. She watched as Addison shook a serious finger at the dog, who was too cheerful to care. Seemed campers had woken up enough to start snapping pictures of the mischievous puppy. "Don't worry, we have way more food left than this crew can eat in a day."

"That your little girl?" Kirk asked.

"Yup." Jeff nodded.

"Precious, aren't they?" The older man smiled. "I have a little granddaughter her age. Catherine, named after my mother. Good solid name, not like those awful modern ones they come up with nowadays." Quinn hid a smile. She'd heard this line a few times before. "Would do anything for her."

"Hey, Quinn!" Marcel was practically jogging through the trees. "I need to talk to you!"

On his unsolved mystery podcast, which was followed by tens of thousands of avid listeners, Marcel came across as serious, focused, and very authoritative. But in person, he was a gangly thin man in his early twenties, with huge round glasses perched on a narrow nose, and the perpetual look of a startled meerkat. Kirk took his leave and wandered over to the coffee. Marcel rushed up to Jeff and even though he was twice half his size, Jeff instinctively stepped back.

The blogger looked at Jeff and blinked. "Who are you and where did you come from?"

"I'm Jeff and I live in an old hunter's cabin about fifteen minutes' walk from here," Jeff said with a tight smile.

"It's not on the map," Marcel said. "I checked very thoroughly and there's nothing around here." For a moment she thought he was actually going to ask Jeff for proof. But instead Marcel turned to Quinn. "You're totally right about which route we should take. I know I tried to twist your arm into taking one of the smaller river branches because, according to my research, there was something totally awesome there you'd want to see. And I promise it would've been totally worth it."

"I'm sure it would've been," she said. "But I can't justify going that far out of our way for a secret something that might be there. Not on this trip. Maybe next time."

"Even if it's about an hour from here as the crow flies," Marcel said.

"An hour by crow but almost four by canoe," she said.

"Fair enough." Marcel grinned. "Also, judging by the clouds and wind, I'm now thinking the rain's going to hit us a lot faster and harder than we were expecting, so the fastest route is definitely the best."

"You have internet access?" Jeff asked. "How? I thought there was no cell phone signal or internet around for miles."

"Oh, I didn't check the weather forecast online," Marcel said. His smile grew. It was large and slightly goofy. "This whole trip is technology free until we get reunited with our phones and laptops at the final stop tonight."

"Although we do have a satellite phone for emergencies and walkie-talkies," Quinn said quickly. "Rose still has the phone actually. It was how I contacted her."

"Unless someone tried to smuggle something in," Marcel added. "It's not like Quinn went around checking everyone's bags for contraband."

"Then how are you checking maps and the weather?" Jeff asked, sounding genuinely curious.

Marcel reached into his back pocket and pulled out a laminated, homemade, spiral-bound flip book.

"I got paper maps," he said proudly. "Weather maps, satellite pictures, old explorer's maps from back in the day, some over a hundred years old. Plus, all sorts of meteorological, geological and geographical data."

An engine roared behind them, growing louder by the second, accompanied by the sound of something crashing its way through the trees. Fearful gasps and startled shouts rose from around them. Voices swore. Immediately Quinn turned to look for Addison just in time to see Rose preemptively scoop her up into her arms and shelter her there protectively, turning the little girl's face away from whatever was causing the commotion. Blinding lights beamed through the trees. A horn blared in a long wail, as if someone was pushing against it.

Then they saw the large black vehicle smash its way through the forest.

"That's Vic's truck!" Jeff shouted.

It broke free from the trees and careened toward the rock cliff. The wheels shot over the edge. For a fraction of a second, the cab seemed to hover midair, and she could see a figure slumped forward over the wheel.

The truck plunged nose-first, free-falling down into the raging river below.

FOUR

"Vic!" Jeff's voice seem to echo in his ears. He ran straight for the water, tunnel vision blocking everything but the sight of his brother's truck wedged nose-first as it slowly sank into the water. The memory smell of the charred remains of his colleagues' trucks three years ago on the other side of the world swept through his mind, along with the pain of its smoke stinging his eyes. No! He wouldn't—couldn't—remember that now.

He forced the memory away, yanked off his boots, dove in and swam for the truck. And immediately he realized his mistake. While there were definitely parts of the river that someone of his strength and size could swim with relative ease on a good day, others were dangerous enough to kill even the strongest person in an instant.

The current hit him full-force, tossing him back and dragging him under. He struggled to the surface, barely gasping a breath before the rapids crashed over him again. His chest ached with the need to breathe. He forced himself to the surface once more and heard Quinn behind him shouting his name.

"Jeff! Take my hand!"

The river tossed him backward into her and they collided like bowling pins. He felt her grab him around the neck in a lifeguard hold. But he wrenched her arm away. No, he wouldn't let Quinn risk drowning to save him from his own mistake.

Then he felt her arm grab him again and this time she held on.

"Jeff, it's okay!" she shouted. "Trust me!"

He felt solid ground under his feet, dug his heels in and pushed himself backward. She let go and they stumbled to shore. It was only then he realized she'd not only stopped long enough to throw her climbing harness back on, she'd anchored it to a tree. He didn't know whether he was more embarrassed he hadn't thought of that or impressed that she had. "Thank you."

"Anytime."

"Where's Addison?"

"Rose took her into our tent, she didn't see a thing." Her words came rapid-fire. "That your brother's truck?"

"Yes," Jeff said. "But I couldn't tell if it was him behind the wheel."

"Okay." She yanked the harness free from the tree. He looked around the campsite and it felt like every eye in the place was staring at him. "Let this be a lesson to all of you that nobody—no matter how strong—is going to have a perfect record against nature. Even the toughest person is going to get knocked down by the wilderness every now and then. Even Jeff. Even me. So right now, I need you all to stay back, let us do our jobs and not try to do anything stupid. We've got this."

"Who's in the truck?" One camper yelled the question everyone must be thinking and Jeff was trying hard not to let overwhelm him.

"Is it Bruno?" shouted another.

Quinn didn't answer. Instead she scooped up two life jackets from a nearby canoe, thrust one at him and buckled the other one on over the harness. "Come on," she said. "If we can't get to him by swimming upstream, we'll just have to go around the other way."

He followed as she ran up the slope, through the tents and along the top of the cliff, past startled campers with a singular and focus. They reached the trail of broken branches and wreckage where the truck had careened from the trees and over the edge. More concerned campers crowded around the edge.

"Stand back!" Quinn shouted.

Jeff looked down at the truck below. It was wedged on a steep angle against the side of the cliff. The vehicle was sinking fast, its front bumper already under water along with half the hood. But the cab was still out of the water.

Please, don't let it be my brother. I need Vic to be okay.

He turned back to see Quinn anchoring the harness to a tree so thick she couldn't get her arms all the way around it and had to blindly throw the rope from one hand to the other. She made it on the first try. Then ran back to him.

"Sadly, we've only got one harness," she said. Then she unexpectedly reached her hand out to his and he stared at it for a long moment before realizing she was waiting for him to take it. "I don't think we should risk losing each other on the way down."

"Agreed." He clasped her wrist and she took his, like one soldier pulling the other out of danger. Determination flashed in her eyes and there was something so unbelievably beautiful about it that it took his breath away.

"Hey," Quinn said softly. "It's going to be okay."

They turned, ran in unison toward the edge of the cliff and leaped. Their bodies fell through the air. He felt her hand slip from his, then half a second later his body hit the water, went under and immediately bobbed back to the surface.

Instantly the current caught hold of him, this time slamming him hard against the bed of his brother's truck.

"Quinn!" He shouted her name and scanned for her in the water. The harness rope disappeared around the front bumper.

"I'm here!" she called. Her face appeared over the other side of the cab. She was clinging to the top of the passenger's-side door. "It's not Vic! It's not your brother!"

Thank You, God! The words flew instinctively through his mind as relief flooded over him, without him stopping to question why a man who didn't believe in prayer was doing it now. He forced his way through the water to the driver's-side door, looked in and started. The body, which was at least a foot too short to be his brother, was slumped forward over the steering wheel. But the disfigured face with its huge hook nose and vacant holed eyes was turned completely toward him. It took a full four seconds for his brain to process that he was looking at a man in a gruesome troll mask.

"Is this who attacked you?" Jeff shouted.

"Yeah," Quinn shouted back. "Bizarre, isn't it?"

Hideous and terrifying more like. No wonder she'd been so confused. The body shuddered a breath. Its head lolled sideways. He heard Quinn barely stifle a scream followed by a prayer of thanksgiving.

"He's still alive!" she cried.

Jeff braced himself against the top of the cab, grabbed the door handle and pulled. "It's locked!"

"This side too!" Quinn called back. "But the window's open a crack. If I take off my life jacket, I should be able to squeeze my arm through."

"Don't. Take. Your. Life. Jacket. Off!" he bellowed.

But it was too late. He watched in vain as Quinn yanked the zipper down.

She could hear Jeff shouting at her to stop and to keep her life jacket on. Something about the depths of the concern in his voice was almost enough to make her stop. Instead, she wriggled her way out of her life jacket with one hand while maintaining a tight grip on the truck with the other. She transferred the life jacket to the same hand holding on to the truck, hitched her body up as high as she could, and squeezed her arm through the small gap in the top of the window. It was so tight, her shoulder ached as her fingers struggled in vain to reach the lock. *Help me, Lord!* She gritted her teeth and fought through the pain until she felt her fingers touch the lock knob and pry it up.

The truck was tilted on a sideways angle toward her and was submerged a good foot deeper on the passenger's side than it was on the driver's. The door unlocked and when she yanked it open, half a dozen empty beer bottles rolled past her, clinking and clattering as they tumbled into the water. The truck stunk so heavily of booze, it was like someone had drenched the seats in beer. She hauled herself into the truck, climbed gingerly across the seat, and pulled the mask off. It was Bruno. His pulse was weak, and he was muttering under his breath like he was talking in his sleep and furiously angry at his dream. She glanced at Jeff through the corner of the windshield. He was shouting up to someone above them she couldn't see.

"Vic's here!" he told her. "Sounds like he was upstairs, saw Bruno steal his truck and drove after him in mine."

Thank You, God!

"Tell him he's alive and semiconscious," she said. "The truck's full of beer and he seems black-out drunk."

Yet as she said the words, she felt the odd niggling at the back of her mind that something wasn't right about the scene.

How had he drunk that many beers that fast? If he'd started drinking before stealing the truck then why were all the bottles in the truck? But she hardly had time to figure it out.

"We've got to put the harness on him and get them to haul him up," she said. "We can't risk taking him downstream if he has any head trauma or internal injuries."

"Don't like it," Jeff said. "But I agree."

Quinn maneuvered her way out of the harness, slid it onto Bruno the best that she could while he limply protested like a cranky, sleeping child. Then she leaned past him and unlocked the driver's-side door for Jeff. He yanked the door open and water cascaded through with such force it would've knocked her backward out of the truck if she hadn't wrapped her hand around the seat belt.

Jeff helped fasten the harness and did a quick check for injuries.

"We should put my life jacket on him too," Quinn said.

"No, we're not—" he started.

"Jeff! Yours is too big and mine will protect his neck and his core—"

"I know!" He cut her off. "And you're right. But what's going to keep you from drowning?"

Her eyes met his and held his gaze for a long unflinching moment. "I've got you."

They slid the life jacket on Bruno and slid him out her side of the truck. Jeff hollered up to his brother and they watched as her co-guide's limp body was slowly hoisted into the air.

"So far, so good." Jeff looked at her over the hood. "Just stay there and hold tight, and I'll come to—"

The truck dropped suddenly, taking Quinn with it. For a moment, she struggled, fighting desperately to get back to the surface. Then she felt Jeff's arms envelop her, pulling her out of the water and clutching her to his chest. She wrapped her arms around him, tucked her head into the crook of his neck and rested in his strength as they spun downriver together.

She felt as jolt as he dug his feet hard into a rock. He staggered to shore, still clutching her. They hit the sand and collapsed side by side on their backs, panting with exertion, his arm cradled under the crook of her neck and her face resting on his chest.

Thank. You. God.

"Hey!" Her sister's voice rose from behind them. "You guys okay?"

"Silly Daddy," Addison chirped. "You don't swim in clothes!"

Quinn rolled over and sat up as Jeff leaped to his feet. Rose jogged down the slope toward them, holding Addison by the hand. She let go of the child, and Jeff swept Addison into a hug. Butterscotch barreled past him into Quinn and quickly licked her face, as if to check that she was still alive, then trotted over to Jeff. Rose repeated what Jeff had said about Vic seeing Bruno stealing his truck and taking off after him.

"He thinks it's a case of potential alcohol poisoning combined with a drug overdose," Rose said.

"Drugs?" Quinn repeated.

"Apparently it'll be next to impossible to get a medevac to land here," Rose went on, "so he's going to drive Bruno to the nearest clinic and see about getting paramedics to meet them on the way."

"Sounds good," Jeff said. He glanced at Quinn. "You mind keeping an eye on Addison while I go talk to my brother?"

"No problem."

Jeff set Addison down and kissed her the top of her head. The little girl ran over to Quinn and flopped down, her head on Quinn's chest as if she was listening to her heartbeat. Butterscotch rolled onto his back beside them and kicked his paws in the air, sending sand flying. Jeff and Rose walked back up the hill.

"You smell wet," Addison said. Her blue eyes looked up at Quinn's earnestly. "You swim too?"

"I did," Quinn said.

"That's silly."

"Very silly," Quinn agreed. She slid her arm around the girl and held her close. Something soft moved through her heart. Addison was such a precious little girl and, thanks to all the chaos, Quinn still had no idea about what had happened to Addison's mother or why Jeff had never talked about her before.

"We need get Uncle Vic's truck out of river," Addison said. "Trucks don't swim."

"Very true," Quinn agreed. She lay back on her elbows and looked out at the water. Any second now, she'd have to head up the shore and talk with the campers. But for now she was thankful for the moment alone with the little girl.

"I'm glad I got to meet you," she admitted, even though she doubted she'd ever see either Addison or her irritatingly intriguing father ever again once they left.

She heard the sound of Vic driving away in Jeff's truck and the thought crossed her mind that he and Addison would now be stranded at their home until Vic returned.

The river surged past her with a pace and ferocity that seemed much faster than it had been the day before. The smell of impending rain hung heavy on the wind. But the group was all experienced canoers and the river wasn't rough enough to justify canceling the trip. If her canoers wanted to avoid being caught in the worst of the storm, they might have to pull over on shore for a while partway through the trip and wait it out. But Marcel had identified a fascinating labyrinth of caves on his map that it might be fun to explore, as long as

they stuck together and didn't venture too deep. Whatever his surprise side excursion was, he'd wanted to
show her, she was sure it would've been fascinating too.

*Lord, I need Your wisdom. Am I going to be able to
continue this trip safely without a co-guide? Should I
try to evacuate them by car?*

It was an eight-hour drive to their luggage and she
had no idea how she'd get enough transport for that
many people up here, but they needed to all be out
of their tents and in an actual safe structure when the
storm finally hit in earnest. She couldn't ask Jeff to help
escort her trip downriver even if she wanted to. And
could she talk him into letting a group of strangers crash
in his cabin when it looked like one person in her group
had attacked her while climbing, tried to break into his
cabin, stolen his brother's truck and crashed it drunk?

The scene of Bruno slumped in the car filled her
mind. Finding him there, in the same mask she'd seen
at the top of the cliff, tied everything up so neatly. Yet
nothing about it made sense. Yes, Bruno had been
known to sneak a flask of vodka onto a trip before.
But multiple bottles of beer? What motive could he possibly have had to attack her, try to break into a house,
steal and crash a vehicle? Would alcohol abuse really
explain all that? And why had Vic said it looked like
he was on alcohol *and drugs*? He wasn't even supposed
to come on this trip and was a last-minute substitution
when her first guide had been in a car accident.

She closed her eyes, ran her hand over Addison's
soft curls and prayed.

Loud and distorted voices seemed to come from
every direction at once. She looked back to see trees

rustling on all sides of the campers. A chorus of some dozen angry, unseen men shouted from within trees, "We have you surrounded! Everybody down! Hands on your head! Now!"

Quinn couldn't even begin to imagine how and why that many attackers were converging on them at once. It felt impossible or even surreal. She saw a man in a gorilla mask step out of the tree line and aim a semi-automatic at Marcel and a trio of female campers. She saw Kirk drop to his knees as a man in a clown mask pressed a gun to his head. Immediately she reached for her satellite phone, before realizing her sister had it. Panicked questions and prayers for God to protect her campers, her sister and Jeff cascaded through her mind. Then she looked down at the little girl in her arms. She had to get Addison away from here.

Quinn leaped to her feet and scooped Addison up into her arms.

"Come on!" she whispered to Addison urgently as she ran for the canoes. "You and I are going to hop in my boat and go for a quick ride, okay? Now I need you to stay really quiet and keep your head down, can you do that for me?"

A woman with unnaturally red hair stepped out of the tree line in front of them. She wore jeans, a hoodie and the mask of a smiling blue puppy Behind her, a painfully thin man with a frog mask aimed a gun right at Quinn.

"I'm here for the girl," she said. "Give her to us now. Or he'll shoot."

FIVE

Quinn held Addison tightly and stood her ground as she stared down the woman who'd just demanded at gunpoint to take the child. The woman's incongruously innocent mask was of the exact same dogs on Addison's backpack. To her right, she could hear the chaos of voices. How many attackers were there? A dozen? More?

"We need to get her out of here," the woman said. "Just hand her over and I'll protect her."

"No," Quinn said. "She's not going anywhere without me." And Quinn would fight to her dying breath to save and protect her.

"Come on!" the frog shouted. "Just grab the kid and let's go."

"No," the woman said. "No violence in front of Addison."

Why? Whose orders were those? Quinn heard a shout and looked up to see Jeff breaking through the chaos above and pelting down the hill toward them. Hope rose in her chest as his eyes locked on hers and she knew, without a doubt, that Jeff would save them.

The man in the gorilla mask charged after him, raised a Taser and fired an electronic dart.

Agony filled Jeff's face as he crumpled to the ground.

Quinn clenched her jaw to keep from crying out and scaring the little girl in her arms.

"Is Daddy hurt?" Addison whispered.

"Yes," Quinn said, "but only a little. He's going to be okay." She knew as she said these words she was prepared to do whatever it took to make sure Addison was safe. The sounds of chaos grew louder among her adult campers. If Addison stayed here, who knew what would happen.

"I'm going with you," Quinn proclaimed. Her voice rose, loud and clear, and somehow to her own ears it seemed to echo around them. "Wherever she goes, I go. You've got orders from someone to keep her safe and happy? I will cooperate with you. But you're not taking her anywhere without me."

The woman looked at the man in the frog mask and then back at Quinn.

"We're the good guys here," the masked woman said. "We're here to rescue her. Nobody's going to hurt her, I promise."

"And you can prove it to me," Quinn said. "Because I'm not going to leave her."

She glanced at Jeff, still lying on his stomach. He raised his head and his eyes locked on hers. His lips moved and, even at a distance, she knew deep in her heart what he was saying. *Thank you.*

Tears rose to her eyes. The puppy-masked woman and the frog-masked man were bickering now. It was clear they were following orders from someone who was very insistent about Addison being happy and protected.

The frog held a satellite phone to his ear with his free hand and said something quickly to the person on the other end that Quinn couldn't hear. Then he put the phone away.

"Fine," the frog snapped. "Big Poppa says we can take her too. But if anything goes wrong, I'm blaming it on you."

The woman reached out and grabbed Quinn's arm.

Quinn allowed herself one long final glance at Jeff's face, then turned and let them lead her into the woods. They walked down a narrow trail, almost single file, and it took her a moment to realize the small rustling sound behind her was Butterscotch following along.

"I'll find you!" Jeff's voice floated through the trees behind them. She hugged the girl closer and knew without a doubt that he would.

"I want Daddy come too," Addison whimpered.

"Me too," Quinn whispered back.

Lord, I have faith in You, in Jeff, and my sister Rose. Please protect them and keep us all safe. In Your name.

The trees parted and then she saw the silver boat. It was small, with a motor on the back that could be lifted out of the water when it got too shallow, and two oars so it could be paddled. The man gestured to it with his gun. The woman stretched out her arms and offered to take Addison, but Quinn shook her head and climbed in with her.

They pushed away from shore.

A yelp burst through the trees.

"Bu'er'scotch!" Addison shouted.

The small bundle of fur leaped into the water and paddled furiously toward them. Quinn set Addison down gently onto the bottom of the boat, leaned over the side, scooped the wet retriever up into her hands, and plonked him into Addison's arms. He wriggled and licked her face as she held him close.

"We're not taking the dog!" the frog said.

"Yes we are, if it makes her happy!" the puppy mask said. "All that matters is keeping her happy."

The current grabbed the boat and tugged it downstream. As Quinn eased Addison's backpack off, Quinn's hand darted into the side pocket, pulled out the clamshell walkie-talkie, and quickly dropped it down the back of her own shirt where it wedged against the small of her back.

The camp grew farther and farther away. Addison began to cry. The woman in the puppy-mask crouched in front of her and reached to pull off her mask.

"Are you stupid?" the man in the frog mask shouted. "Did you forget we took a hostage. You really going to let the person we kidnapped see your face?"

"Addison is scared!" she shot back. "Our most important job here is to keep her happy! That's why he got me to be the one who picked her up."

The woman pulled off her mask. She was younger than Addison would've expected, barely more than twenty, with a round, ordinary face and worried eyes.

"I care about her," she added. "Even if you don't."

The woman turned to Addison.

"Hi, Addison," she said in an unnaturally cheerful, singsongy voice. "Do you remember me? Kelsey, your teacher from preschool? We're going on an adventure today, like the ones we used to go on together at school. I brought all your favorite snacks and treats, and coloring books, and even some activities for us to do."

Addison's tears stopped. Her face rose to the woman, confusion filling her eyes. "Hi, Kelsey. Where we going?"

"On a fun adventure," Kelsey said brightly. "Now, I brought a special life jacket just your size. Once we put it on, you can have a cookie. I brought your favorite chocolate chip."

Addison let Kelsey help her into the small pink-and-blue life jacket, which Quinn noticed had the same puppy pattern as Addison's backpack and the woman's mask.

Kelsey beamed a relieved smile over her shoulder at her partner.

This wasn't a kidnap for ransom or a crime of opportunity. These people knew Addison. They'd come prepared and, despite how much they claimed they wanted to keep her safe and happy, somehow Quinn knew wherever they were taking her, they intended that she'd never see her daddy again.

Jeff lay facedown on the forest floor with his hands tied behind his back. The smell of damp Ontario earth and pine needles filled his senses. Residue pain from the Taser he'd been shot with still buzzed through his limbs. The sound of his own heart beat so loudly, it filled his ears. Interlaid over the world around him, like an old double-exposed photograph accidentally merging two scenes into one, memories from three years ago and half a world away also swept over him. He remembered the searing heat on his skin and the blinding of the sun beating down from a cloudless, oppressively bright blue sky. He could hear voices shouting in a language he didn't understand as the almost painful stretch of burning rubber and oil filled his senses.

He closed his eyes so tightly they hurt. *God, I don't know if You're real or not. And if You are, if You'd even want to listen to me. But my little girl's been kidnapped. Quinn's with her, and people are in trouble around me. We're in desperate need of Your help.*

"Pssst!" a voice hissed urgently. "Jeff!"

He opened his eyes, looked around, and couldn't see where the voice had come from. A small group of campers was down on the ground off to his left. Through the trees, he could see a handful of others straight ahead. Despite hearing over a dozen voices in the trees, he could only see two hostage takers—one in a gorilla mask and one in a clown mask—pacing between them all, like they were uncertain of what to do next. He'd seen far better organized kidnap and hostage attempts overseas. Once, in the desert, he and three colleagues had been briefly kidnapped by a group of youths, barely more than teenagers, and held for less than an hour before being rescued by an American patrol. It had been a tense and eye-opening experience. They'd been young but efficient and focused.

By comparison, these guys seemed to have no idea what they were doing. Like someone had ordered them to tie people up and wave guns at them, without explaining why.

Was all this just a diversion to allow Paul to snatch Addison away from him? But why and how would man who'd been led to believe he was Addison's rightful father go to such extremes?

"Jeff!" The urgent whisper came again. It sounded female, close by and louder this time. He looked at the dense foliage above him and saw nothing but leaves.

He heard something small fall through the branches. Then the object hit him hard right below his shoulder blade. The man in the gorilla mask turned toward Jeff and raised his weapon. The unseen item slid off Jeff and onto the ground. Jeff moved his elbow over it to keep anyone from seeing it. The man in the gorilla mask went back to pacing back and forth between trees.

Jeff rolled to his side and reached for the mystery item. He winced as something sharp pricked his finger. It was a pocketknife. He glanced back at the trees and still couldn't see who was up there, but whoever it was, they'd been smart enough to open the knife just enough that he could roll onto his back, nudge the blade between the plastic zip ties and then push it the rest of the way open with his body weight. He rocked his body from side to side. The blade sliced through the ties and his hands snapped free, making him wonder just how sharp the mystery knife had been.

The man in the gorilla mask turned back toward him. "Hey! What are you doing?"

Jeff threw himself at the man, knocked him down and pinned his back to the ground before he could even get off a shot. Then Jeff grasped the gun and wrenched it from his hands. He yanked the Taser from his belt as well. It only held two shots, and both had already been spent. Then he leaped to his feet and aimed the gun down at the masked man.

"Who are you working for?" Jeff demanded. "Where have they taken my daughter?"

"Hey! No!" the man shouted. "It's not what you think!"

Jeff glanced at the weapon in his hand and growled under his breath. While the Taser had definitely been real but the gun was fake. The gorilla scrambled to his feet, turned and ran blindly into the woods. Something crashed through the trees above him. He leaped back, as Quinn's sister Rose tumbled to the ground in a shower of leaves. She landed on her hands and knees but in a second was back on her feet.

"Give me my knife," she said. "I'll cut people free while you take them out."

He hesitated for a second and was about to tell her to run and hide before realizing that Quinn's sister was probably every bit as stubborn as she was.

He dropped the knife into her outstretched hand. "This gun was a fake and the Taser is out of charges. I don't know about the other men's weapons, though. How many hostage takers did you see?"

"Four," she said. "The two who took Quinn and Addison, and the two who waved guns at us, which doesn't make sense because I heard about twenty voices."

"Same here," he said.

"Stay safe," she said, her dark, serious eyes making him think of her sister.

"You too." He turned and ran in the direction the man in the gorilla mask had disappeared. He heard people shouting and screaming, Marcel telling someone to "run this way." Don telling someone to stay down, and Kirk yelling that the clown's gun was also a fake.

Then the trees broke, and he saw the man in the gorilla mask leaping on an ATV. So that was how they'd come through the woods. But why was there only one vehicle? The motor revved. The man in the clown mask crashed through the trees ahead of him.

"Come on, man!" The gorilla shouted. "We've got to go!"

They were bailing—even faster than the young mercenaries on the battlefield had when they'd seen the American troops coming.

The clown leaped on the back of the ATV.

Jeff sprinted after them, pushing himself as fast as he could, but he lost them through the trees.

Panting, he bent over and grabbed his knees.

They were gone, and he was no closer to finding his daughter and Quinn or getting them back.

"Yeah, we'll never catch them on foot," Rose said. "Maybe if we still had a vehicle. But Vic took your truck and his is still in the river."

Did she think he needed a reminder?

But as Jeff turned and saw Rose walking up behind him, the depth of worry in her eyes made him check himself before he said the words out loud. Campers staggered behind her like survivors from a disaster film.

"I've done a complete head count," she added. "Everyone's accounted for. Except for your daughter and my sister. No major injuries." She glanced to the sky. "Thank You, God."

Addison and Quinn were just kidnapped, and she was thanking God? Unbelievable! She was just as bad as his brother.

Rose reached into her camping vest, pulled out a satellite phone and offered it to him. "I don't know who to call. Do you even have 9-1-1 out here?"

"Yes, but it patches through the local RCMP who will take a couple of hours to get here," he said.

He took the phone, called both the RCMP and his brother Vic. The RCMP said they'd send people to evacuate the campers, start a search for Amber and Quinn, and put out an Amber Alert.

Vic told him that Bruno was drifting in and out of consciousness and promised he'd rush back immediately to help with the search the second he got Bruno to doctor or paramedic. Jeff ended the calls and turned back to Rose.

"My cabin is a less than twenty-minute walk from here," he said. He pulled his keys from his pocket and tossed them to her. "Just follow this road until you see a tire tracks heading to the right. I need you to take the campers there, lock the doors and wait for rescue. It's fully stocked with food, heat and running water. When you get there, I want you to head straight for the kitchen, get the satellite phone on the counter and use it to call me on this phone and my brother. His number's on the fridge. Sorry to swap phones but it'll be a lot faster this way and we have no time to lose."

"And where will you be?" she asked.

"I'm going after Quinn and Addison."

She threw the keys back and he caught them. "I'm going with you."

"So am I!" Don stepped forward from the group of campers. "You'll need backup."

"I'm coming as well," Kirk said. The old man's arms crossed.

Right now Jeff had to nip this in the bud before he had a convoy of a dozen people trailing along behind him.

He gestured Rose farther away from the others and stood with their backs to the campers.

"What were you doing up in that tree?" he asked.

"Well, there were these bad people with masks and guns," she said with a feeble attempt at a joke. But when she searched his expression, her smile faded. "My dad always taught us that when you're in danger you should run, and if you can't run you should hide, and if you can't hide, you should fight. It sounded like we were surrounded, so I hid."

Seemed Quinn wasn't the only Dukes sister he'd underestimated.

"My dad was a single father," Rose said. "He raised us in the middle of nowhere and was pretty convinced our lives were in danger because of some trouble he'd been involved in before we were born. We were home-schooled and taught skills like running, climbing, hunting, shooting, archery, knife skills, foraging—all the survivalist stuff. Also, baseball, hockey and lacrosse. We lost all kinds of projectiles in the woods behind our house."

He opened his mouth and, for a moment, had no words. "I had no idea," he said finally.

"Well, my sister's a pretty open book," Rose said, "unless you give her a reason not to trust you. There's nobody better for your little girl to be with right now."

"If you're proficient with a knife, why did you throw yours to me?" Jeff asked. "You don't know the first thing about me."

"You kidding me?" Rose asked. "Do you have any idea how big an impact you had on Quinn or how much she talked about you? She wrote me so many letters back when you guys were working together, going on about how incredible you were. She really looked up to you, even though your grumpiness drove her nuts. If Quinn trusts you, that's good enough for me."

Wow.

"And Quinn trusts you," Jeff said, "and I trust Quinn, which, at the moment, makes you the only person I can trust. Right now we have a dozen scared and traumatized people in the middle of nowhere who need to get to safety. Somebody needs to take charge of the situation, take these people to my house and keep them safe until rescue comes."

Rose closed her eyes. Her lips moved in silent prayer, and he watched as peace washed over her features.

"And it has to be me," Rose said. Her eyes opened.

He handed her the keys and this time she took them. As she turned and walked to brief the group, he slipped away, running through the trees to the river before he had a fresh round of volunteers to contend with. He got to the canoes, chose one, and had started loading it with supplies and a life jacket for Quinn when he saw Marcel's gangly form running through the woods toward him.

"You're not coming with me and I don't have time to argue," Jeff said.

"Then take this." Marcel pressed his flip book of laminated maps and charts into Jeff's hand. "I've charted all the rivers and caves and marked off all sorts of things that might be helpful."

Jeff swallowed hard. "Thank you."

Marcel threw his arms around him in an awkward but genuine hug. "Just bring them back safely, okay?"

"I'll do my very best."

Jeff turned, put a life jacket on, and pushed the canoe out into the water, leaping in just as the current grabbed hold. He started paddling and, in moments, the silence surrounding him was filled with only the sounds of the river and the forest.

After twenty minutes, Rose called to tell him they'd reached the cabin and she'd secured the phone. Moments later, Vic called to tell him Bruno's condition was worsening and the Canadian Rangers were mounting both a ground and helicopter search for Addison and Quinn. He also reminded him that due to the impenetrable foliage and terrain, it might take hours to find them, so it was vital Jeff did everything in his power to figure out where they were and pass that information on.

"But has Paul been arrested yet?" Jeff prompted. "You know how he threatened to get Addison back by any means necessary."

"A detective buddy assured me that police are looking into him—"

"He did this!" Jeff said. "I know it."

"And if so, they'll prove it and he'll face justice," Vic assured him. "In the meantime, I'm praying for you, and people are out in force looking for Quinn and Addison."

They ended the call and Jeff continued paddling, following the current and, whenever he hit a fork, taking the branch it would be easiest for a motorboat to go along. His ears strained in vain for the sound of voices or the kidnappers' tin boat.

Almost half an hour had passed before the phone rang again. There was no name on the call display but he answered it anyway. "Jeff here."

"Oh, I know who you are." The voice was male, deep and raspy. "And I know what you've done."

"You won't get away with this," Jeff said. "I will find you."

The man laughed. An ugly and menacing sound that sent anger surging like lava through Jeff's veins.

"Where are my daughter and Quinn?" Jeff asked.

"Addison is safe," the man said, "but Quinn won't be unless you call off your dogs—"

"Look, Paul—if it's you…" Jeff said. "It's not my fault Della did what she did—"

"This is not about her!" the man shouted. "It's about you, Jeff! Don't follow me. Don't look for me. Don't send anyone after me. Because if I hear so much as a boat on the water, a voice in the trees, or a helicopter in the air, I will not hesitate to kill every single person you claim to love, and their deaths will be on you."

SIX

Dark clouds gathered overhead. Quinn guessed she'd spent almost two hours sitting on the cold metal floor of the motorboat, with Addison leaning against her legs and Kelsey crouched in front of the small child, trying to fill the time with games, treats, activities and songs. Her artificial cheerfulness was desperate and creepy but at least it was helping distract Addison from being afraid, although she'd never stopped asking for her daddy. Quinn was also thankful they'd brought a life jacket for the little girl, leaving Quinn as the only one on board without one.

Kidnapping her hadn't been part of the plan.

The frog had pulled off his mask when the wind picked up, showing the pale face of an agitated, young, curly haired man underneath. Kelsey had called him "Benny" in a flash of frustration and the growing shake of his limbs showed he was used to having some kind of illegal substances coursing through his veins and was now in withdrawal, either because he hadn't been able to replenish his drug supply or had already taken everything he had the second he got it. A lot of addicts didn't have either the money or discipline to have extra drugs on hand for later. He'd be in a hurry to get back to his dealer.

She'd watched and listened long enough to know both Kelsey and Benny were afraid.

But why? And of who?

Mostly, Quinn kept her mouth shut and prayed. She prayed for Addison, for Jeff, for the kidnappers, for Vic and for Bruno. She prayed for herself and for everyone involved in the rescue effort. She asked God to take care of each one of her campers by name. The responsibility of caring for each person on her trip weighed heavily on her heart—as if they were her chicks and she was the mother hen—along with the guilt of not doing a better job at protecting them.

Was this her fault? Was there something she could've seen or done to stop all this from happening? Even if she made it out alive, she was sure this would be the final trip she would ever lead. Her dream of running a wilderness adventure group was over. Her company had been struggling financially before now; rather than the trip that would gave her the boost to rescue her business, this would be the one that ended it. She prayed God would ensure every single camper entrusted in her care would get home safely.

Words from Psalm 46 filled her mind.

God is our refuge and strength, a very present help in trouble. Therefore will not we fear, though the earth be removed, and though the mountains be carried into the midst of the sea. Though the waters thereof roar and be troubled...

Thick raindrops began to fall, splattering all around

them. Addison whined and whimpered, "No wet! No like wet."

The boat bounced against submerged rock, one of many Benny had collided with as the river grew rougher and spun. Addison complained loudly.

Kelsey turned to Benny and shouted at him to keep the boat steady.

"How about you keep the kid quiet," he snapped.

"She just doesn't like the rain," Kelsey said.

"So, I'm supposed to control the weather now on top of everything else?" Benny said. He waved a hand toward Quinn and the dog. "None of this was the plan."

What was the plan? And whose plan was it?

"Why don't you just pull over and we can wait until the rain stops?" Kelsey asked.

"How about because we're supposed to meet Big Poppa tonight?" Benny shot back. "And I don't exactly want to anger him by not making it or getting stuck spending the night in the woods!"

The small boat hit another rock.

"I'm asking Big Poppa." Kelsey grabbed a satellite phone from her pocket that looked far more expensive than either of them could afford. She texted a quick message to an unseen number. A moment later, the phone beeped. She smiled like an angry cat while Benny's face paled. "He wants to talk to you. Pull over, I'll take Addison into the tent to get out of the rain and you can explain to Big Poppa how you can't drive a boat straight."

A tense silence fell. It took a full fifteen minutes before they saw a narrow fork in the river jutting off to the right. Benny steered them into it and beached the boat.

Kelsey picked Addison up in her arms with an overly cheerful announcement about just how much fun setting up a tent was going to be. She tried to carry a bag, the dog and Addison all at once before giving up and letting Addison and the dog walk.

Minutes ticked by and everything inside Quinn ached to follow them. Then, finally, Benny slung a small but heavy-looking bag over his shoulder, ordered her out of the boat, tied her hands behind her back with a bungee cord and marched her through the trees. It was only the fear of what might happen to Addison if she ran or Benny shot her that kept Quinn from fighting back. They passed a tiny pink-and-blue pup tent that matched everything else Kelsey had bought for Addison. Kelsey's voice filtered through the trees, trying to convince Addison they were on a special adventure and to get her to sing.

"She won't hurt her," Benny said. "We're here to rescue the kid."

"From who?" Quinn asked. "From a good father who loves her and would do anything for her?"

"You're so dumb!" Benny snorted. "I'm not the bad guy here. You don't know anything about that kid, her parents or her life. Trust me, she'll be much better off where she's going."

Quinn pressed her lips together. To a degree, he was right. She'd never even known Addison existed until that morning and still didn't know who her mother had been.

But she knew without a doubt that Jeff had a good

heart, he loved his daughter, and that they didn't deserve to be torn from each other's lives.

They reached a clearing. Steep rocks rose out of the ground around them. "Now, I'm going to tie you to that tree, climb up there to get a better signal and make a phone call. Keep calm and cooperate, and I won't have to hurt you."

And here he was protesting he wasn't the bad guy.

She turned her back to the tree. He looped a bungee cord around her waist fastening her there.

"Who's Big Poppa?" she asked.

He didn't answer.

"Why are you so convinced you're the good guys?" she persisted.

"Be quiet," he said. "Or I'll gag you."

He left her there and walked up the rocks, stopping every now and then to check the phone for a signal and wave it around over his head. Rain pattered on the leaves above her but, between leaping into the river twice and being caught in the boat in the rain, she'd reached that level of dampness where she didn't really feel it anymore.

She heard Benny swear a few times and then he yelled, "Hello? Hello? Hi! Yeah, it's me. Are you whispering? I can barely hear you!"

She rolled her back against the tree and felt the small clamshell walkie-talkie digging into her. She breathed a prayer of thanksgiving and eased her hands up the tree until she could pry it out. So far, so good. Then she inched her body down the tree while moving her arms up, trying to get her bound hands as close to her mouth as possible. The bungee cords dug into her skin.

Her legs ached from the effort of supporting her weight, and she was reminded of that painful squat exercise that involved leaning against a wall and pretending to sit in an invisible chair. When she had her hands up as high as they would go, she wedged the clam shell into her elbow, switched it on, and prayed.

"Hello?" she whispered as loudly as she dared. "Hello? Can anybody hear me?"

Static hissed.

"No!" Benny shouted so loudly and suddenly, Quinn nearly dropped it. She froze, thinking he'd spotted what she was trying to do. But when she looked up, she realized he was yelling into the phone, pacing, swearing. "I don't kill people! You get that, Big Poppa! I'm here to rescue some kid. Not kill some random lady and hide her body in the woods!"

"Hello?" Jeff's voice was faint, but it still sent relief coursing through her. "Is somebody there?"

"Jeff!" she whispered. "It's me. Quinn! Addison is okay and safe for now. But I think they're about to kill me."

Jeff pulled his canoe to a stop against a rock. Water rushed past him, buffeting against the sides of the boat. Feelings he couldn't begin to put into words surged through him. He needed to find Quinn, to protect her, to cradle her in his arms and know that she was safe. His heart pounded so hard at the sound of Quinn's voice it was like it was trying to escape from his rib cage and soar to wherever she was.

"Is Addison okay?" he asked. "Where are you?"

Nothing but silence and static filled his ears. "Quinn? Can you hear me?"

He couldn't have lost her already!

"I'm here." Quinn's voice was back in his ear. "Addison is okay. They haven't hurt her."

Palpable relief crashed over him like a wave. So many questions rushed to the tip of his tongue that, for a moment, he was unable to speak.

"I'm tied to a tree with the walkie wedged in my arm and might only have a few moments alone before they come back," Quinn said. "But I'll stay on the line for as long as I can. Again, Addison is alive and okay. She hasn't been hurt or threatened in any way. If anything, the kidnappers are trying to shield and cocoon here from the reality of what's happening." She was talking quickly, like she was worried each word she spoke might be her last. "One of the kidnappers is named Kelsey. She's about twenty, shoulder-length red hair. Apparently, Addison knows her from day care?"

"I know her," he said. "She'd become overly attached to Addison and tried to get close to me. Made me really uncomfortable."

And evidently his instincts were right. His mind searched for a last name and came up with Drew. Kelsey Drew.

"She's with a partner," she said. "A boyfriend maybe? Young and fidgety. Named Benny."

"That's her brother," he said. "Addicted to pain meds, has a criminal history. Dabbled in some other drugs too."

"That would explain why he has the shakes."

"Their dad died of a heart attack a few years back,"

Jeff said. "It's pretty tragic. He was only in his late forties and serving in the military. Shocked everyone, according to Vic. Their uncle took them in. He's Vic's pastor, and Kelsey was briefly Addison's daycare teacher."

That now gave them another suspect of who was behind them. Despite how much Vic respected his pastor, he'd just hit the number-two slot on Jeff's suspect list after Della's former fiancé, Paul.

Jeff wedged the clamshell walkie-talkie in the crook of his neck, pulled out the satellite phone and texted Vic rapid-fire.

Quinn called on walkie-talkie. She and Addison are alive. Kelsey and Benny Drew are the kidnappers. Will call ASAP.

"How are my campers?" Quinn asked. "Are any of them hurt? Are they safe and accounted for? Is my sister all right?"

The depth of her worry for the group she'd been leading permeated her voice. Even kidnapped and tied to a tree, her concern was for her campers. Something about that made Jeff's breath tighten in his throat. How had he never seen how impressive she was?

"Yes," he said. "Every single camper is safe, unhurt and accounted for, including your sister. The people who ambushed us fled and she's taken everyone to my cottage. Rose has been checking in with me regularly on the walkie-talkie. Everyone's okay."

"Where are you?" he asked.

"I don't know. They pulled off onto a small stream

on the west side of the river and climbed up a slope. He tied me to a tree, so he could make a call to his boss. They call him Big Poppa. Apparently, they're meeting up with him tonight to hand over Addison."

"I'll talk to Vic, and they'll set up police blocks at the mouth of the river and local towns," he said. "Have they hurt you?"

"No, I'm fine," Quinn said. "For now. But I think Big Poppa's on the phone right now, telling Benny to get rid of me."

"Who else is with you?" Jeff asked.

"Nobody," she said. "Just Kelsey and Benny. Oh, and Butterscotch is safe with us too."

That should be a big relief to Addison. But none of that explained the mysterious phone call he'd received.

"Who called me and threatened me?" Jeff asked. "It was a man. He had a deep voice."

"No idea," Quinn said. "It wasn't either of them. Neither has been out of my sight until just few minutes ago. I guess it was Big Poppa. What did he say?"

"That if he saw so much of a glimpse of a helicopter or ground search, he'd kill everyone I love," Jeff admitted.

It had seemed so intensely personal. Like Big Poppa knew him, had a grudge against him, and wanted him to suffer. Was it Paul, the man who'd thought he was Addison's father? He'd definitely had reason to threaten Jeff and had done so before. Or was it Pastor Drew, the charismatic church leader who taken in his niece and nephew when his brother died? He had a clear link to the kidnapping. While Jeff had never been to his church and didn't know the pastor well enough to have an opinion, Vic was convinced he was a good man. So why would he be after Addison? Was there some link between Paul and Pastor Drew that Jeff wasn't aware of? How would they even be connected?

She didn't reply right away. A long pause stretched out on Quinn's end of the line, where all he could hear were indistinct scuffling and breathing sounds.

"You still there?" he asked.

"Yeah, just thinking," she'd said and, considering how desperately she'd scrambled to get her words out just moments earlier, something about the fact she was now pausing made an uncomfortable feeling build inside his gut.

"What about Addison's family?" she asked. "Who are they? What are they like?"

There was an edge to her voice bordering on suspicion. Heat built on the back of his neck like it was suffering the rays of an unrelenting sun. Della's face swept unbidden across his mind. "They're not a part of this."

"How could you possibly know—"

"Her mother's dead," he said. "She was an only child. Her grandfather has never been in the picture and her grandmother is the kind of sweet lady of faith that prays for Addison daily and sends us Christmas and birthday cards."

"How did her mother die?" Quinn pressed.

"Look, I'll tell you all about her another time," Jeff said. *She didn't love me. She didn't like me. She thought I was garbage. And it's my fault she's dead.* "But right now we've got way more important things to worry about."

"Kelsey and Benny think they're the good guys…"

"It doesn't matter what they think—"

"What if it does?" Urgency permeated Quinn's voice. "They're calling this a rescue mission. They came prepared to take Addison. They got her a life jacket, snacks, toys, a tent—Kelsey even picked her mask to resemble something she knew Addison would like. Benny called me stupid when I told him that Addison had a good father who loved her. He said I knew nothing about her life."

All the words he should have spoken before and all the secrets he'd been keeping from Quinn about Addison buffeted his core like the water smacking against his canoe, threatening to drown him.

"Jeff, I don't think this was a crime of opportunity or they set out to abduct some random kid," Quinn went on. "I think this is personal. This is about you and Addison."

"And I'm telling you not to worry about that, please," Jeff said. He gripped the walkie-talkie so tightly, he could feel the plastic start to buckle.

"But—"

"Look, Quinn—" he cut her off "—there's a man out there who thinks he's Addison's real father. His name is Paul. He's not her biological father and he never raised her. Addison lived with her grandmother until she was one and then she came to live with me. But the police are already looking into him. That's what I think this is all about and who I think is behind this. But again, police are on it. So for now, just focus on staying alive and know that I'm coming to get you."

"What is that?" a voice he vaguely recognized as Benny's shouted down the line.

"A plastic toy," Quinn said.

"Give it to me!" Benny snapped.

Jeff listened helplessly to Quinn yelp in pain as Benny wrenched it from her grasp.

Please, God, if You're listening, help her now. Whatever I've done or whatever You think of me, Quinn doesn't deserve to bear any of it.

"Hello?" Benny shouted into the walkie-talkie so loudly, it squealed with distortion. "Listen to me. Whoever you are, you've just signed this lady's death warrant. I'm going to take her, and hurt her, and kill her, and hide her somewhere you'll never find her. And it will all be your fault!"

"No!" Jeff shouted. "Wait! Don't!"

Quinn screamed, sending shocks of pain through Jeff's heart.

"Quinn! I'll find you!"

The walkie-talkie went dead.

Help me, Lord. What have I done?

He grabbed his phone.

"Hello, Jeff?" Rose answered before it had even rung once. "Good news on the evacuation front. A friend of a friend has a place for us three hours away in Muskoka. So we're saved the eight-hour drive—"

"Rose, your sister and Addison are alive," he interjected. "I'll explain when I can. But right now I need you to put Marcel on the phone—urgently."

"Okay," she said.

The line went silent. Seconds ticked past.

"Hello?" Marcel asked. He sounded nervous.

Jeff held up the laminated flip book the young man had compiled as if he could see it through the phone.

"If you were going to kill someone and hide their body in the woods so that nobody ever found them, what would you do?"

SEVEN

Benny stomped the plastic clamshell walkie-talkie into the earth and then ground it to smaller and smaller pieces under his foot, destroying her only way to communicate with the outside world.

"You're not going to kill me," Quinn said calmly and slowly, like she was trying to convince a wild animal not to strike. "You're the good guy, remember? You're on a rescue mission. You're not a killer. You don't hurt people. That's not the kind of person you want to be."

An angry, thin-lipped smile crossed Benny's face that terrified her.

"I think it's time for you to shut up," he said. He started riffling through his bag.

Lord, please help me get through to him before it's too late.

"Benny, wait," Quinn said. "Whatever this is, you don't have to do it. You don't have to take orders from Big Poppa or anyone. Or let someone turn you into someone you don't want to be."

He pulled a roll of silver duct tape from his bag.

A chill ran down her spine.

"I know you love your sister, and she loves you too,"
Quinn went on, throwing out every word and argument
she could think of to save her life. "I know you lost your
father a few years ago to a heart attack, and that you
have some problems, but your uncle took you in. He was
military just like Jeff. He wouldn't want this for you."

"You don't get to talk about my father," Benny
snapped. "He was a hero and nothing like Jeff." He
tore out a long strip of tape and she heard the adhesive
slowly rip away from the roll. "You don't know anything about him or me."

"Maybe not," Quinn said. "But I do know that no
matter what you've been through, there's hope for you.
There's a whole world of faith and love out there, waiting to give you the opportunity to change your life,
shake your addictions, and start anew."

He yanked the strip free of the roll and started toward her.

"Please, Benny!" she pleaded. "It's not too late. You
can still walk away before you do something you can't
ever go back from."

"I warned you what would happen if you didn't
stop talking." He didn't even look at her as he shoved
his elbow against her throat, pinning her in place. She
barely had a second to pull her lips in to protect them
as he stuck the duct tape firmly over her mouth, muf-
fling her ability to scream. "Now don't fight me or I'll
make this worse than it has to be. I just want to get this
over with."

He undid the bungee cord fastening her to the tree,
grabbed her by the shoulder and steered he away from
the tree in the direction of the boat. With the other hand,

she felt him press the barrel of the gun against the small of her back. Then the sweet sound of Addison singing filtered to her through the trees. Tears filled her eyes, swamping her vision, and she had no way to wipe them away. The rain had all but stopped now. It wouldn't be long before they packed up camp and moved Addison. If he shot her here, Addison would hear the blast and be traumatized. But her death would also leave evidence that investigators might be able to use to find the little girl. It was a risk Quinn was willing to take.

She prayed hard for God's help. The gun dug deeper into her back.

"Walk," Benny barked.

She stumbled a step then pitched forward, falling face-first toward the ground. The gun slipped from the small of her back. At the last second, she tucked in her neck and tumbled into a partial somersault, wincing as the full impact of the ground struck her shoulder. Yes, disarming a man with a gun when she had both hands tied behind her back would be near impossible. But so was pulling the trigger for the first time when you'd never killed anyone before.

She rolled onto her back and heard the safety click off. But it was too late. She kicked up wildly and made contact, sending the gun flying out of his hand.

Benny swore and leaped on her, knocking her head backward into the ground. Pain flooded through her skull. The sickly sweet scent of chloroform flooded over her. *Oh, no. Please no.* If he couldn't bring himself to shoot her, he'd drug her first. She tried in vain to gasp a breath through the tape that gagged her mouth.

He pressed a wet rag over her nose. She thrashed

from side to side even as she felt the nausea and dizziness sweep over her, dragging her deeper and deeper into unconsciousness.

Help me, Lord. Save my life. Save my sister Rose and the other campers. Help Jeff find Addison and bring her home safely. Bring into their lives the love they deserve...

The darkness swept over her before she could finish her prayer.

Quinn drifted in and out of consciousness, not knowing which nightmares were in her chloroformed dreams and which were real. She heard the sound of Benny shouting to Kelsey that Big Poppa would be late meeting them in town. And that Big Poppa had told him to go stash Quinn somewhere where she'd never be found to slow down investigators.

Then she felt herself being dragged and lifted into the boat. The metal floor of the boat shook beneath her, tossing her back and forth. She heard water gurgling past her ears and felt cold drops of rain sting her skin. But always, just as she thought she was about to wake, nothingness would fall over her again.

Help me, Lord. She had no idea how long she'd slept, drifting in and out of fleeting glimpses of the world around her, or even when she'd started to wake up. The first thing she knew for certain was that her body ached and sharp stones were digging into her back.

She opened her eyes and saw nothing but pitch-black darkness. The air was cold and clammy, but the wind was still and no rain was falling from the sky above. A slow, relentless, dripping seemed to echo around her.

Nausea swam over Quinn. She rolled onto her knees, stretched her mouth as wide as she could, and desperately rubbed the corner of the duct tape against her shoulder. Thankfully, it peeled free, no doubt dirty, wet and dusty from her ordeal.

Quinn gasped a breath, tasted damp and stale air, and realized she was in a cave. No doubt one of the deep labyrinthine ones Marcel had shown her on the map. She knelt upright and struggled against the bonds holding her wrists. She strained her ears in the darkness and heard nothing but the sound of her own ragged breath.

She was alone. Benny had apparently decided against pulling the trigger himself and had left her here to die. Fear seized her chest. Her heart beat so loud, it deafened her.

"Quinn!" She heard Jeff's voice calling her name. So faint and far away, she wondered if it was only in her imagination. "Are you there? I'm at the mouth of the cave. If you can hear me, follow the sound of my voice. Look for the light!"

"Jeff!" she screamed his name into the darkness with all her might, she braced herself against the wall and pushed to her feet. "I'm here."

An explosion shook the air, like a crack of a whip or the detonation of a bomb, somewhere over the top of the rock wall above her. Then came the roar, like a landslide of rocks cascading down the tunnel as the roof caved in ahead of her. She turned and tried to run, stumbling deeper and deeper into the darkness, trying to keep ahead of the cave-in before it buried her alive. She tripped and fell, tumbling to the ground.

A light flickered from behind her. "Quinn!" Jeff

shouted her name in the darkness. Then she felt his strong hands reach for her, grab hold of her body and lift her into his arms. "It's okay. I've got you."

Jeff cradled her to his body and kept running, deeper and deeper into the cave, keeping one step ahead of the rocks as they caved toward them. He stumbled and pitched forward. She nearly fell from his arms. But he held tight and took the brunt of the impact as they crashed against the ground. His light went out. Rocks pelted down upon them. Dirt poured like rain. Jeff wrapped his arms around her, shielding her with his body.

Finally, it was over and silence fell again.

Jeff sat up slowly and pulled her to sit with him. She felt his fingers yank the bungee cords from her hands. She reached for him in the darkness and felt his face under her fingertips.

"Jeff, is it really you?" she asked.

He chuckled softly. The flashlight switched on again and she saw his handsome face just inches from hers.

"Yup, it's me," he said. "Live and in person."

"Have you found Addison yet?" she asked.

"No, not yet." Sadness pooled in his eyes. He opened his mouth but no words came out. Instead, he just shook his head.

"I'm sorry," she said. She wrapped her arms around him and held him for a long moment. Then they slowly pulled apart. "What was that?"

"Some kind of explosion," Jeff said. "Either some kind of bomb with a remote detonation device or someone fired what's called a high explosive incendiary weapon at the cave. We'd need to get experts out here to know for sure."

He reached into his pocket, took out his satellite phone and dialed.

"They've issued warrants for Benny and Kelsey's arrest," he added, "and pulled their uncle and aunt in for questioning."

He looked down at the phone and frowned. "The signal is so weak that nothing's getting through."

"We're probably too far underground," she said. "How long has it been since I was knocked out?"

"It's been almost an hour and a half since we talked on the walkie-talkie," he said.

An hour and a half? She gasped a breath that sounded part whimper and part sob to her own ears. How had they stolen so much of her life?

"The good news is we're alive and we're together," Jeff said. "The bad news is that we've been buried alive."

Dust filled Jeff's lungs. He stood slowly, reached for Quinn's hand and helped pull her up to her feet. Then he shone the flashlight around them. The ceiling was barely an inch above his head. The tunnel was so narrow, they could barely stand side by side. A wall of rocks and rubble lay where the exit had once been with a deep dark tunnel on the other side. His ears still rang from the explosion. The smell of smoke seemed to linger in the air, and he couldn't tell if it was from whatever had caused the cave-in or his memory playing tricks on him again.

"My best guess is that whoever Benny is working

for didn't want the people tracking them to find your body too easily," Jeff said.

"He said it was to slow down the investigation," Quinn said.

"Sounds about right," he agreed.

Could also because he'd known Jeff would be tormented by the question of what had happened to her.

What caused this place to explode and cave in?" Quinn asked, as if reading his mind.

"I don't know," he admitted. "The area was absolutely deserted. Nothing strange and nobody in sight. Definitely no sign of explosives. I only knew you were in here because the ground was scuffed and it looked like someone had dragged something through the underbrush. I walked into the cave and started calling for you. Suddenly there was a bang and the cave started to collapse. I heard your voice, and I ran for you."

He wondered if it was only the fact that Quinn was there, he'd been focused on her and had held her in his arms that had kept the memories of the past at bay.

Her hand brushed his arm. "How did you find me here?"

"I called Marcel and asked him where he'd hide a body," Jeff admitted.

"And he sent you to this cave?"

"Actually, this was the third one I tried," he said. "Apparently this one's the most dangerous and you wouldn't agree to adding it to the trip."

"So we're in Bear's Paw?" she asked.

"Yeah, something like that."

She blew out a long breath and turned toward where the tunnel disappeared into the darkness. "Then we can't go that way," she said. "It'll just get narrower and narrower until we'll be crawling on our hands and knees. And no matter what branch we take, we'll never find our way out."

Suddenly, Jeff felt his chest tighten as if the walls were closing in around him. Panic reared like a monster inside him. His lungs struggled for air. Each breath felt more painful and shallower than the last. He needed to get out of there. He had to run. He couldn't be trapped.

Then he felt Quinn reach for his hand. She looped her fingers through his and squeezed tightly.

"Hey, Jeff, it's okay," she said. She pressed her other hand gently on his chest, like she was feeling for his heartbeat. "Just focus on my breath, okay? Listen to me breathe, in and out, in and out. Then try to match me when you can."

He nodded, his throat feeling too tight for words.

For a long moment, they stood there, side by side, her hand holding his. Silence fell between them in the darkness, punctuated only by the sound of her slow, steady breathing and his own ragged gasps. Then slowly, finally, he felt his heartbeat begin to relax and the air return to his lungs.

"We will find her," Quinn said. She dropped her hand from his chest, but didn't let go of his hand. "I have faith. You will bring her home safely and I will do everything in my power to help you make that happen. I promise."

And he knew with absolute certainty that she meant every word she said.

"You're sure they won't hurt her?" he heard himself ask.

"I'm positive they don't intend to," Quinn said. "Kelsey was spoiling her. Like I keep saying, they think they're rescuing her."

From him. From the man Addison's mother Della said was such garbage he didn't deserve to be anyone's husband or father. His hand flinched in hers as if expecting her to let go. But when she didn't, he felt his fingers relax into hers again. His thumb ran over the side of her hand.

"Thank you for going with my little girl and protecting her," he said. "You are the most incredible person I've ever met, Quinn. You're brave, fearless, and have shown me far more kindness and compassion than I've ever deserved. I think the fact you were also really pretty kept me from seeing who you were on the inside. I'm sorry."

She pulled her fingers away from his and blinked. Now why had he just admitted that? Quinn ran both hands through her tangled hair with an awkward laugh.

"Well, that was before you'd seen me half drowned, dragged through the brush and buried alive," she said. "Maybe I should be thankful there are no mirrors in the wild."

"You look fine..." he started to say. Then he realized he was already so far over his skis he might as well admit what he was actually thinking. "Honestly, you look amazing, considering everything."

She smiled mildly and turned toward the wall of rock penning them in.

"And now you have me worried we're already running out of oxygen," she said. "I can't tell you how tempted I am to just rush deeper into the caves, looking for a way out, but my brain is telling me that if we do that, we'll just end up wandering around in circles until we die. If Marcel's maps are right, and he's not secretly part of this too, the only way out is to tackle this wall of rock and dig our way out."

She brushed past him and her shoulder touched his, sending a warmth through him.

"You're not the only one battling back the panic down here," she said. "I've never been a fan of enclosed spaces or feeling trapped. I tried to work an office job once and something about being in a cubicle all day made me feel like I wanted to jump out of my skin. Like I told you, when I was a kid, I used to climb out of my bedroom window at night."

"Until you fell and broke your ankle," he added.

"Oh, I still tried to climb down a rope ladder with my broken ankle in a cast." An odd laugh that was a cross between a chuckle and a giggle slipped her lips. "I might be great with heights, but the truth is, I'm more than a bit claustrophobic. So, while it sucks for you that you're trapped here, I'm really glad you're here with me and I'm not alone."

"I'm glad too."

She dug her fingers into the wall of rocks and started pulling them loose one by one. He joined her and together they dug their way out one stone at a time. They worked shoulder to shoulder. It was slow, tedious work, pulling each piece of free and throwing it down the tunnel behind them. Some of the rocks and earth fell free easily. Others were so wedged in by the weight of the rubble pressing on top of them that, even with their combined effort, it took a painfully long time to wriggle them free. Every now and then their work would bring a cascade of more dirt and stone pouring in on top of them, filling the hole they'd just created, erasing all their hard work and pushing them back even deeper into the tunnel than they'd been just moments before.

Still, they kept digging. And despite the pain and the fear weighing down his heart, there was something about having Quinn there that kept Jeff from surrendering to it and completely unraveling. In the past, it was like he hadn't trusted in her positivity and optimism, thinking that it was either an act or she was hopelessly naïve. Back then, it was like he'd been so angry at the world, his ears and eyes had been shut to seeing how happy a person could really be. Now he was open to seeing her as she really was—optimistic, plucky, cheerful and filled with a hard-to-define lightness that brought strength and energy to her movements.

It was comforting and beautiful in a way he couldn't put into words.

They worked side by side in silence for so long, he hadn't even realized he'd started singing to himself under his breath until he heard his own voice bouncing off the walls at him. He stopped as heat rose to his face. What's worse, the song was just some silly and empowering pop anthem that had been everywhere back when he'd been in high school. It was the kind with a catchy beat, a lot of "nah nah naaaaaahs" and lyrics about believing in yourself.

"I'm sorry," he said, "I didn't realize I was doing that."

"Don't stop on my account," Quinn said. "You can totally keep going. I was kind of enjoying it."

He stopped digging. It was impossible to tell how much actual progress forward they'd made. But looking back, he could see the mountain of rocks and rubble they'd left in their wake. The tunnel that had spread out behind them had completely disappeared, leaving them completely trapped between two walls of rock.

"I would've sung along with you," Quinn said, pulling his attention back to the task in front of them, "but I didn't know the words. I was eleven or twelve when that song hit it big. And my sisters and I were home-schooled until high school. We lived in this big, huge farmhouse in the middle of nowhere. There was no radio signal, except CBC sometimes. And I mean CBC news, not even the cool new Canadian music shows. We definitely didn't have a television, although my dad took us to the drive-in every now and then in the summer. But my dad had a record player with all these amazing folk-type songs from the fifties, sixties and seventies. So, if you sing something old, I'll join you. I had Bing Crosby's version of 'Don't Fence Me In' running around my head for a while, but figured it was a bit too on the nose."

He chuckled and it surprised him that here, trapped underground in the darkness with the knowledge his little girl was in danger, Quinn had somehow lifted his heart toward hope. Like it was a tiny and stubborn boat being lashed on a great storm of pain, fear and sadness without being dashed to pieces.

"Your sister told me some about your childhood," Jeff said. "I completely forgot to tell you this, but she actually hid up a tree when the kidnappers struck, and then threw a knife down at me."

Now it was Quinn's turn to laugh softly.

"I had no idea that your dad was so..." His voice trailed off as he floundered for the exact word Rose had used.

"He raised us to survive," Quinn supplied. She turned back to the walls and kept digging. "I definitely don't blame him for never falling in love again after my mom died. But raising four daughters alone in the middle of nowhere definitely took a toll on him. He was always worried that someone might break in and hurt us, because of some stuff that he and my mom had gone through long before I was born.

"My mom died when I was tiny. And Dad raised us like he was preparing for a zombie apocalypse or something. He taught us everything—hunting, fishing, climbing, foraging for food, building a fire, purifying water for drinking, and both tying knots and escaping from them."

She pulled a handful of tiny rocks from the wall and tossed them behind her.

"Rose said something similar," Jeff said. "Also, sports."

"Yeah." She smiled. "I'm a decent first baseman. But my real passion is wilderness stuff like climbing and canoeing."

"I had no idea," Jeff said. "Your childhood sounds intense."

"It was sometimes," Quinn said. "But he really, really loved us. There was never a single day in my life when I doubted that he'd do anything for us. Plus, he told really amazing tales. We prayed, we sang songs and made up stories together. He also taught us breathing exercise and how to just be still. The ability to just still my heart and be in the moment has got me through a lot. Do you find singing helps you with anxiety?"

"I don't have anxiety," he answered reflexively. He was surprised how dismissive and defensive his voice sounded to his own ears.

"Oh," Quinn said. "I'm so sorry. I thought you were having a panic attack earlier."

When Bruno crashed his brother Vic's truck into the water and he'd rushed into the water without pausing to check the current? When the masked men had snatched his little girl? Or earlier in the cave when she'd held his hand and helped him breathe? The question crossed his mind but he stopped himself before he asked it. After all, did it really matter?

"I don't have panic attacks," Jeff said, flinging the words out as if the sheer force of his will would make them true. "You sound like Vic. My brother thinks I have PTSD—post-traumatic stress disorder."

Now, why had he confessed that?

"Do you?" Quinn asked softly.

"No," Jeff said. "I don't know. But he keeps nagging me to see someone about it, like a psychiatrist or a therapist. He said he heard about this trauma survivor's group that meets once a month in Kilpatrick—"

"My sister Leia's fiancé attends that group," Quinn said. "Jay's a detective. Used to be undercover, investigating a pretty nasty serial killer. That's how he and Leia fell in love."

"I thought being in groups like that was supposed to be anonymous?" Jeff asked.

"Maybe for most of them." Quinn shrugged. "But

Jay told us to tell anyone we thought might be helped by something like that. There are a lot of cops in it, actually, but civilians too."

She wasn't looking at him. Instead her gaze seemed completely focused on the task of digging them out one handful of dirt at a time. And he found himself wishing that she was up in his face, telling him that he was wrong and challenging him directly, like his brother Vic did, so he had something to argue against.

"Well, Vic also wanted me to go to his church and talk to Pastor Drew because he thought we'd really connect," he added, like he was verbally shadowboxing the big brother who wasn't even there. "That's the same Pastor Drew who I expect is currently sitting in a police station with his wife, because the niece and nephew he took in after their father died tried to murder us and are currently on the run with my daughter."

Quinn nodded and for a long moment didn't say anything. Finally, she asked, "What do you think they meant by telling me that they were the good guys who were rescuing Addison?"

Her voice was gentle and kind. Like someone carefully opening up a wound to clean and heal it. But still, her tone didn't stop the sting.

"I have no idea," he said. After all, he knew why Della's former fiancé, Paul, thought he had reason to abduct the little girl he'd once been told was his biological child. But he had no idea if that had anything to do with Kelsey and Benny's motivation. It's not like he'd interrogated the members of the Drew family or had any proof they were connected to Paul and the threats he'd posted online.

But just as he found himself rationalizing why he was within his rights to keep the incredible woman he was currently trapped in a cave with completely in the dark about the worst parts of his past, he could hear another small part of himself arguing that he was tired of running and hiding. He wanted to open up his heart. He wanted to unburden himself and be known.

"Quinn, there's this whole big part of my life surrounding Addison that I don't like talking about," Jeff said. "I know you probably think it's weird I never told you about her when we were working together, although, to be fair, I only found out she was my daughter just before I quit. And I guess there's no excuse for letting you believe she was Vic's daughter this morning and refusing to answer your questions earlier when you were literally tied to a tree. But it's embarrassing, and humiliating, and personal."

"So's the fact I was homeschooled by a survivalist in the middle of nowhere," she said. "I'm not saying for one second it's the same thing. But my childhood was so religious and focused on all this wilderness and survival stuff that nobody in my high school could relate to it. I was the weird kid who didn't know anything about pop culture. In grade eleven, a classmate asked me what I thought of some movie star and I asked what class he was in."

"You're right," Jeff said, "it's not the same thing."

"I know," she said. "I also failed most of my classes because I couldn't sit still, and I never went to college or university. And back when we worked together, I was already so worried that you thought I was dumb,

I was terrified of what you'd think if you knew I only had my grade twelve."

"I never thought you were dumb—"

"All I'm saying is everyone's broken," Quinn said. "We've all got weird and damaged things inside us, just in different ways."

"Addison's mother Della never loved me," Jeff said, forcing the words he'd never told anyone out of his mouth with a gasp like he'd just surfaced for air after holding his breath under water for far too long. "I'm pretty sure she never even liked me."

"I'm sorry," Quinn said. "That's horrible."

"I cared about her so much," Jeff said. "At least, as much as it's possible to care about someone who never loves you back. Vic says the feelings you start a romantic relationship with is like a seed—the potential of what it could be. In which case, mine never got to grow because it was always one-sided."

"I'm so sorry," Quinn said again. "My sister Sally went through something like that with her daughter's father. A few people I know have."

He took a step back. He'd been all alone in his own world of pain for so long, it was almost unnerving to hear Quinn so casually state that he was hardly alone. And maybe if he hadn't been trapped in a cave digging his way out, he'd have left it there. Maybe he'd have shown her just the tip of the iceberg and never even hinted at everything else lying under the surface. But he realized he was angry—at everyone and everything, but most of all at himself—that he couldn't keep it hidden any longer.

"She hated me." Jeff stopped digging and turned to

face Quinn. "Her mother said it was because I reminded Della of her controlling, manipulative and abusive father who she'd blocked from her life as a teenager. But I don't really know. I mean, what makes a person chose to be in a relationship with someone they don't even like?" His voice rose and his words echoed around him. Then his shoulders sagged. "And how do I live with knowing that I was the bad choice she made?"

"I don't know," Quinn said softly. She dropped the rock she'd just pulled free at her feet and ran her hand up his back, letting it rest between his shoulder blades. And, for a moment, it was the gentle pressure of feeling her there that was the only thing that kept him from falling.

"I had no idea she'd had a fiancé back home," he went on. "The guy named Paul I told you about, who the police are looking into now. When I found out she was pregnant, she told me and everyone that Addison was Paul's daughter. And I believed her. I didn't even try to figure out the math, because I never even suspected she was lying. Della not only put Paul's name on the birth certificate, she'd told him that if anything ever happened to her, he should apply for a restraining order to keep me from Addison. Because I'd only end up hurting her and my little girl would be better off without me."

"Jeff…" Quinn started, and something about the kindness and affection in which she'd just said his name was enough to bring unshed tears to his eyes. "You have to know that's not true. Whatever Della did or said was because of her own pain. It has nothing to do with you."

"Are you sure?" Jeff asked. He turned to face her

and they stood there in the gloom of the tunnel, his face just inches from hers. "What if Della was absolutely right about me? What if I never should've taken the DNA test and then filed to get custody of Addison when I found out she was mine? What if I'm wrong to be out here looking for her and fighting to bring her back home? What if I'm never going to be good enough to be her father, Big Poppa is right, and she's better off without me?"

EIGHT

Quinn's heart jolted as suddenly and painfully, as if someone had literally sucker-punched her in the chest. She grabbed Jeff's hands and held them tightly, not even stopping to notice they were still full of dirt.

"That's not true," she said. "Every word of that is a lie. Your daughter adores you. I saw it in her face and I saw it in the way you look at her. And most of all, I know the kind of man you are.

"Any person in their right mind would be so incredibly blessed to have you in their life—as a father, a friend, a brother, a partner on the battlefield, and yes, even a husband. I'm sorry for everyone who ever said those horrible words to you and even sorrier that part of you keeps replaying and believing them."

Her hands dropped his and slid up the sides of his face, not even stopping to think she might be leaving even more muddy streaks along the strong lines of his jaw. "Don't believe the lies, Jeff. Please. I know who you are. God knows who you are. And you are worth so much more than that."

He wrapped his arms around her and pulled her to

him. She leaned against his chest, her fingers reached around his neck, and he felt his heart beating into hers.

"Love is supposed to make you feel better about yourself, right?" he asked after a long moment. "Stronger? Better? Like you can do more and be a better person, right? That's what Vic says."

I wouldn't know, she thought. *The only man I ever felt anything for was you. And that seed, or whatever it was, was never even planted let alone given the opportunity to grow.*

Before she could even try to find words to say, he let her go and turned back to the wall that imprisoned them.

"Trying to care about someone the way I loved Della, when they don't care about you, kills something inside of you," Jeff said. He grabbed hold of a boulder twice the size of a pumpkin and tried to yank it out. It didn't move. He stepped back and kicked at the edges of it, breaking through the dirt until he had enough space to get a better grip. "Whatever I felt for Della was toxic. It left me sick to my stomach. Like I was slowly poisoning myself."

He dug his fingers around the huge bolder again. She reached out to help him pry it loose, but he waved her off. So she busied herself with scooping out some of the smaller rocks and dirt that surrounded it.

"I guess I should be thankful our relationship only lasted a few weeks," he said. "We were never close. Never friends. And yet, when I found out she was pregnant, I scraped some money together, drove to the closest mall to the barracks and bought her an engagement ring. I told her I'd support her and raise her child.

Thankfully, she refused to marry me. But she didn't have to be so rude and nasty about it."

Quinn's arms ached to hug him again, just like she'd held him moments before. She wanted to embrace him, rest her head on his shoulder and stroke the silky brown hair at the back of his neck. Instead, she watched as he rammed his fingers even deeper into the small crevasses he'd made along the edges of the stubborn boulder and yanked. It budged. He rolled it slowly out of the way, one painstaking inch at a time. Dirt and rocks rained down in the space it had left behind.

"Della's family held a memorial service for her almost a year after her death, because bringing her body home from overseas took time and her mom wanted to hold it during the summer and also give everyone who cared about her time to fly in for it," he went on.

"You told me she was dead," Quinn said. "But you've never told me how she died."

"She died while serving overseas," Jeff said. "I'm not ready to go into all the details of that. It's a bit more than I can handle talking about right now."

That was the second time he'd brushed her off when she'd asked him about his daughter's mother's death. Maybe that was one stone he wasn't yet ready to turn over because he wasn't sure he could handle what was hiding underneath.

"I was working with you at the time of her memorial," he told her. "I'm not even sure why I went. I was lurking in the back of the church when her mother spotted me and practically made a beeline for me. She pulled me aside and told me the truth. That Addison was my daughter. She told me that Della had confessed she'd been seeing someone in the unit and that the timeline didn't match up with the ultrasounds, but that Della had insisted Paul should think he was the father. She explained that Della's estranged father had also been a military man, but a really bad guy. Charming, but manipulative and really controlling. She said I shouldn't blame myself that Della had been attracted to me and pushed me away."

He shoveled dirt with his hands.

"Della's mom was amazing," he said. "She'd been the one raising Addison and had always suspected the truth. Paul, on the other hand, was apoplectic. So overcome with anger, he couldn't see straight. He tried to block the DNA test. When that failed, he tried to sue me. And when that didn't work, he sent me email after email threatening to take Addison away from me. He even started this online blog drumming up sympathy. I was genuinely worried he'd show up one day and take Addison."

"Is that why you moved up here and installed a security system at your cabin?" she asked.

He turned and smiled at her as if he'd almost forgotten she was there. "You know, I think that's the longest I've ever heard you go without chiming in or asking a question."

She snorted. "Well, if it's any consolation," she said, "I have plenty of words running around in my head right now but I don't think hearing me pepper you with personal questions or scream about how you don't deserve any of this will be particularly helpful."

He chuckled too. It was a sad sound, but a hopeful one.

"For what it's worth," he revealed, "Vic thought Paul was all bark and no bite. But that pressing charges against him would be the kindest thing I could do. Because it would make him wake up, realize how out of control things had gotten and, hopefully, get him help for his pain. Vic is a nicer person than I am sometimes."

"Why didn't you press charges?" Quinn asked.

"Because I wanted to pretend the whole thing wasn't happening and to hide until it went away," he said. He reached up and grabbed a wide slab of rock by the ceiling. "Okay, I'm going to need a second pair of hands for this one. Can you get the other side?"

"No problem."

She reached up on her tiptoes and took hold of the other side. They wriggled it free, going back and forth and taking turns pulling. Finally, it fell loose. Late-afternoon sunlight trickled through.

She turned to Jeff and saw the relief and joy bubbling up in her heart reflected there in his eyes.

"Well, Miss Quinn Dukes," he said. "I think we've found ourselves a way out." He kicked the huge boulder he'd done battle with back to the wall, stepped up on it and looked through the hole. "The rain has stopped, and the coast is clear."

He reached his arms through and pulled himself out of the cave. A moment later, his face reappeared in the gap. He reached down, grabbed hold of her arms and helped pull her out and onto a huge pile of rock and rubble where the cave mouth had once been.

Quinn gasped a deep breath, thankful to feel fresh air fill her lungs. Prayers of thanksgiving surged through her and unexpected tears rushed to her eyes.

Jeff sent a quick message to Rose, then dialed Vic. When Vic didn't answer, he left a message and put the phone back in his pocket.

"Thank you for saving me," Jeff told Quinn. His voice was deep and husky with emotion.

She turned to him. "Are you kidding?" she asked. "You saved me!"

He swallowed hard, as if searching for words. Then he gave up and instead wrapped his arms around her and pulled her into a hug.

"Sometimes the memories and the pain get the better of me," he whispered into her hair. "It feels like it's all too much. But when you're there, it's better. Plus, you listened to me without judging me. It helps to know I'm not alone."

"You're not alone," she said.

She tucked her head into the crook of his shoulder. Her hands slid up the strength of his back. She felt his jaw brush against the top of her head. Warning bells sounded in the back of her mind. How many times would she find herself hugging this man before she found her heart trying to turn their relationship into something more than it was? They were two people who'd been thrown together in an emotional pressure cooker. They were both scared. Neither of them was thinking squarely. And she'd already gotten her feelings all tangled up in this man before and only ended up hurt. Yes, people who were close sometimes clung to each other in times like these, when pain, relief and fear all kept colliding into one. But not people who barely knew each other. Not people who were going to leave each other's lives as soon as this was over.

Not people who she knew had no future together.

It wasn't just because of all the stuff Jeff was wrestling with and the fact he needed to face it all and begin to learn to stop hating himself before he could ever build a healthy relationship with someone else. Although that was definitely a huge part of it.

But it was also because she knew that while she'd never ever regret the decision she made to be kidnapped alongside Addison and leave her campers behind, what was happening now was still just a small slice of time away from her real life. She had a job running trips with a company that had been in financial trouble before this started. God had not only entrusted her campers into her care, she felt like her whole heart was inspired toward fulfilling this dream. That was her real life. Not this terrifying, confusing moment she was trapped in today. Or the unforgettable man she was trapped in it with.

"I'm sorry," Jeff said.

"You have nothing to apologize for," she said.

"Yes, I do," he said. "I don't like how hard I was on you when we worked together. It's like I couldn't stop testing you and prodding at your façade like I was trying to prove you weren't really as great as you seemed to be. I never consciously took what happened between me and Della out on you. You're absolutely nothing like her. But…well…you know you're…well, you're dazzling, right?" *Dazzling?* She pulled back just far enough to look up into his face. "You've got this almost magnetic way about you that just draws people in. Quinn, you're beautiful."

So first he'd called her pretty, then dazzling and now beautiful?

"But I didn't want you think of me as beautiful," she said. "Or pretty or dazzling or whatever word you come up with next. I wanted you to respect me as an equal. I wanted you to admire my skills and not the way I looked. I wanted you to like the person I was and what I brought to the table as a colleague."

Her voice rose. But she hadn't moved away. She was still there, perched precariously on the rocks they'd just dug their way out of, tucked inside his arms.

He blinked. "You think I didn't like you just because I was hard on you?" he asked.

"You were *way* too hard on me—"

"I agree," Jeff said, "and I was wrong. I apologized for that, and hopefully I haven't treated you like that since."

No, he hadn't. He'd listened, followed her lead at times, and completely respected her. Plus, he'd actually taken full responsibility for being difficult to work with in the past and hadn't tried to deny it, gaslight her, excuse it or wave it away.

They hadn't even been back in each other's lives a whole day…

"And yes, of course, I liked you," Jeff sputtered. "I more than liked you. I liked you more than anyone I'd ever met."

Hang on, what was he saying? And why was she letting him talk to her this way?

It was like there was this current, invisible and strong, that kept pulling her toward him no matter how hard another part of her kept pushing away.

Jeff leaned forward, she did too, and she felt his forehead rest against hers. For a long moment, neither of

Treat Yourself to Free Books and Free Gifts.

Answer 4 fun questions and get rewarded.

◀ **DETACH AND MAIL CARD TODAY!** ▶

	YES	NO
1. I LOVE reading a good book.		
2. I indulge and "treat" myself often.		
3. I love getting FREE things.		
4. Reading is one of my favorite activities.		

TREAT YOURSELF • Pick your 2 Free Books...

Yes! Please send me my Free Books from each series I select and Free Mystery Gifts. I understand that I am under no obligation to buy anything, as explained on the back of this card.

Which do you prefer?

❑ **Love Inspired® Romance Larger-Print** 122/322 IDL GRDP
❑ **Love Inspired® Suspense Larger-Print** 107/307 IDL GRDP
❑ **Try Both** 122/322 & 107/307 IDL GRED

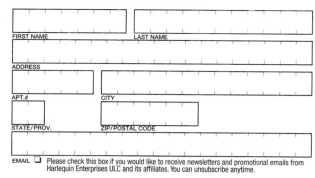

FIRST NAME   LAST NAME

ADDRESS

APT.#   CITY

STATE/PROV.   ZIP/POSTAL CODE

EMAIL ❑   Please check this box if you would like to receive newsletters and promotional emails from Harlequin Enterprises ULC and its affiliates. You can unsubscribe anytime.

LI/SLI-520-TY22

them said anything. They just stayed there, resting in the closeness of being safe and together, and breathing each other in. Then he felt his hand reach under her chin and tilt her face up to his. Her eyes closed.

Jeff's phone rang. The loud trilling seemed to shake the space between them. He let go of her, yanked out his phone and stepped away so quickly she nearly tumbled backward into the hole.

"Vic!" he shouted into the phone. "You have no idea how amazing it is to hear your voice! I've found Quinn. She's alive and safe." A wide smile beamed across his face as he spoke her name. "But we—" His smile vanished as his words stopped. "Uh-huh, okay. Hang on, I'm going to put Quinn on speakerphone so she's part of this too." He sat on a thick ledge of rock and waved for her to join him. As soon as she was seated beside him, he held the phone between them and pressed the button. "Okay, I'm with Quinn now and we're on Speaker. Tell her what you just told me."

"I'm sorry to tell you that Bruno's passed away," Vic said.

A sharp but inevitable pain moved through her. "So was it alcohol poisoning or drug overdose? Or was there something else he took or that someone administered to him?"

She'd known the scene in the truck had looked suspicious. There was no way a vodka drinker would take that many bottles of beer on a canoe trip or for the mere fact he was drunk make someone act so irrationally. A lot of people drink without breaking into houses, stealing trucks or committing crimes.

"None of the above," Vic said.

"Then what?" she asked.

"Somebody just shot him."

The confusion Jeff watched wash over Quinn's features was only matched by the downright befuddlement of his own. Bruno had just been shot. Murdered. After getting drunk, first surviving crashing Vic's truck into the river and then surviving nearly drowning. Quinn's face paled, her skin went white and she dropped her head forward between her knees.

"I'm sorry," she said. "All of a sudden I feel really sick."

Jeff rubbed her back between her shoulder blades.

"What happened?" Jeff asked. "What do you mean somebody just shot him? Where? How? Who?"

Vic took in a deep breath and blew it out.

"It's been a busy few hours, so forgive me if I go over anything I've told you before," Vic said. "Bruno's vitals were good when we lifted him out of the river. He'd been drinking but I wasn't convinced that was the only thing going on. I wasn't about to go into details then with a crowd of people standing around, but I suspected there was something more in his system too."

Quinn raised her head and Jeff pulled his hand away.

"You mean like illegal drugs?" she asked.

"Prescription painkillers actually," Vic said. "They'd explain why he was so sleepy and out of it. It wouldn't take much for someone to crush up some pills and mix them in his beer."

"He usually drank vodka," Quinn interjected. "But that's a clear liquid and beer's brown. Plus, it doesn't have as strong a smell as beer."

"That tracks," Vic said. "Bruno floated in and out of consciousness as I drove him to the clinic. He'd wake up and cry or rant and then pass out again." The disgust in his brother's voice was unmistakable. "It was pretty pathetic. I also had to pull the truck over a couple of times because he was sick. But I got him to drink a whole lot of both water and sports drinks. So, I was optimistic he'd sober up and be able to tell us what conceivable reason he'd have for doing what he was doing. I also blared Ontario Christian radio when I got into range and made sure he got a full blast of both rocking worship music and teaching." Vic chuckled softly at the memory.

Yeah, that sounded exactly like the kind of thing his brother would do.

"Obviously, I was incredibly careful about everything I said on the phone to law enforcement, Rose and you, because I knew he'd be able to listen in," Vic went on, his voice sobering. "Not sure if it was the conversation he overheard, the radio I was blasting or his own conscience kicking in, but the more of the drugs and alcohol he got out of his system, the worse he felt about everything. He was pretty incoherent. But he said he met someone online who somehow knew about some fraud he'd committed and money he'd gotten as a result of it. Something to do with claiming he'd been injured on a previous trip when he'd actually been drinking. Called him Big Poppa."

Jeff felt Quinn grab his hand and squeeze it hard.

"Did he tell you anything about him?" Jeff said. "Anything at all?"

"No," Vic said. "I wish I'd pushed him to tell me

more, but he was really incoherent and I thought we had time. I called the police, asked them to meet us at the Kilpatrick clinic, and told them Bruno was willing to give them a statement. The police were there, waiting for in the parking lot, when we arrived, along with a nurse all ready with a gurney and a hydrating IV. Bruno had dozed off again. Like I said, he was in and out a lot.

"I got out of my door, started to walk around to his side and then suddenly heard gunshots. Like a sniper was hiding in the trees, peppering the lot with gunfire. Everyone hit the deck. When the shooting stopped, Bruno was dead. Somebody had shot him right through the passenger window."

Pain filled Quinn's heart. She prayed that Bruno had sought peace and forgiveness before he'd died.

"Did they catch the guy?" Jeff asked.

"Nobody even saw who fired," Vic said. "Police cordoned off the whole area and did a complete perimeter, but didn't see so much as a footprint."

Jeff frowned.

"I found Quinn in a cave just as we theorized," Jeff said. "As soon as I entered it and started calling for her, it collapsed and we had to dig our way out, which was why we were unreachable for so long. But just like your invisible shooter, I didn't see anyone explode the cave either, so I'm guessing I hit some trigger I didn't see."

How could he protect himself and the people he loved against an invisible enemy?

"Oh, that reminds me," Vic went on. "I told you that along with putting out warrants for Kelsey and Benny, they pulled Pastor Drew and his wife in for questioning, right?"

"You did," Jeff said. "Do you think it's possible your pastor had anything to do with this?"

"No, I don't," Vic said bluntly. "I think both he and his wife are good people who took in his dead brother's very troubled children. But I've also lived long enough to know I can't always assume I'm right about people and things."

Yeah, Jeff thought, wasn't that the truth.

"Have they found Paul?" Jeff asked.

"No," Vic said, "apparently he'd been off the grid for a few days, along with his girlfriend and parents. But they have arrested two men suspected of the hostage taking at the campsite this morning. They still had the gorilla and clown masks with them and confessed pretty quickly. They claim they were paid a lot of money to wave fake guns around, Taser anyone who got out of line, and tie people up, and that somebody told them it was just a harmless stunt for a viral video. I believe the first part, not sure if I believe the second. They claim it was a two-man job and there was nobody else with them."

Quinn sat straight and looked at Jeff. "But I heard more than two people. There were people coming in every direction. You were surrounded."

"I thought so too," Jeff said.

"So does everyone else questioned," Vic said. "People claim to have seen anywhere from ten to twenty masked men with guns. How many did you see?"

"That I know I saw for certain?" Jeff asked. "Just two. I heard more than two voices. I saw the trees moving in multiple places at once." Jeff blew out a breath. "You ever hear the adage that when you feel water on your skin you don't need to see it actually fall from a cloud to know it's raining?"

"No," Quinn said. "But I know the principle of Occam's razor—the simplest solution is almost always the best."

"*Almost* always," Jeff repeated. "And the fact we have an invisible gunman and an invisible detonation, the idea of invisible hostage takers sounds a little less impossible. Not that it gets us any closer to finding my daughter."

"We have every major mouth of the river blocked off and every town they could possibly leave from has roadblocks," Vic said. "Plus, we have helicopters in the air for aerial search, and ground teams. But we'll have to call those off when the storm picks up again. They're forecasting dangerous winds with the risk of tornadoes. We've got every realistic way out of the forest covered but, honestly, they should've exited by now. So they must be hiding out somewhere."

Quinn's eyes rose to the horizon and he watched as her lips moved in what he suspected was silent prayer. Then she stood and started to walk a couple of steps away from them down the mountain of rock. She stopped. "I overheard Benny say something when I was drifting in and out of consciousness—"

"Hang on." Concern filled the military medic's voice. "Why were you unconscious? Are you okay now?"

"They used chloroform," Quinn said. "I slept it off. But I should probably hydrate."

"You should," Vic said. "Take it slowly."

"I will." She glanced at Jeff and smiled. "Benny and

Kelsey said they were meeting up with Big Poppa tonight in a town. I don't know what town it is."

"Again, we have every town covered," Vic said.

"Unless there's a town we don't know about," Quinn said.

Jeff watched as an idea formed in her eyes. "Vic, can we call you back?"

"Sure," he said. "By the way, I'm heading to the cabin now to help with the evacuation of the campers. It took a lot longer than we'd hoped. But that's because when word began to spread through our communities and prayer networks that you all were in trouble, apparently a friend of a friend of your sister Leia's detective fiancé offered everyone rooms in a motel of theirs only three hours away and they needed some time to get them ready. They even arranged to have everyone's luggage and belongings driven up so everyone will have their stuff."

Quinn closed her eyes and prayed. "Thank You, Lord."

They ended the call and she asked Jeff to call the cabin.

"Hello?" Rose's voice was on the line even before it had time to ring once.

"Hey, it's me." Quinn's voice was suddenly tender. "I'm okay."

"Oh, thank You, God!" Rose praised.

"Jeff's here with me," Quinn added. "You're on speakerphone."

For a moment, Jeff heard the soft sound of Rose sobbing in relief. Then she said, "Everyone—I mean absolutely everyone we know—has been praying for you. Do you have Addison yet?"

"No," Quinn said. Tears glistened in her eyes, but her jaw set with determination. "But we will soon, I have faith. Can you put Marcel on the phone for me?"

"Absolutely," Rose said.

There was a pause then Marcel came on the line. "Hello?"

"I hear I owe you one," Quinn said.

A deafening whoop echoed down the line. "I was right?"

"You were," she told him.

"You were in a cave!" Marcel exclaimed.

"I was," she said. "Now, I need you to be right again and about something even more important. Are you alone?"

"I can be," he said.

Jeff heard footsteps on the floor and then the sound of his sliding kitchen door opening and closing. "I am now."

"Okay, we have reason to believe the kidnappers are hiding out in a town," Quinn said. "Is there any way there's a town, or a village, or an outcropping of buildings anywhere near this river that I don't know about?"

There was a pause then Marcel said, "There might be a ghost town."

She glanced at Jeff and he felt fresh hope fill his core.

"Where?" she asked.

"Page thirty-nine," he said. "It's marked with a gold star. It's the surprise detour I wanted to take if we had time. I don't know for sure what's there. But one of the old surveyor's maps I found in the national archives said there used to be a big mill there, and I saw something in the satellite maps that looked like buildings."

"Thank you," she said. "Don't tell anyone what you told me, okay? Nobody at all. Not even my sister. We can't risk the possibility one of the other campers you're with is somehow mixed up in this and overhears you."

"Okay," Marcel said. "Do you want me to hand you back to your sister?"

"No," Quinn said. "Tell her I'll call her back when I can."

Jeff ended the call. "Do you think we can trust him?"

"I don't know," Quinn said. "But I do think this is the best chance we've got for finding your daughter and bringing her home alive."

NINE

They called Vic back and gave him the rundown of everything Marcel had told them.

"I'm going to the cabin to help get all the campers out of our living room and on their way to the motel," Vic told them. "Then I'm going to join in the search for Addison. Hopefully, this potential ghost town checks out."

Quinn watched as Jeff's brow crinkled.

"Whoever the criminal is who called and threatened me earlier," Jeff said, "he said that if he saw any glimpse of a helicopter or ground search, he'd kill everyone I ever loved." He blew out a hard breath. "And I don't know what to do with that."

"What do you want to do about it?" Quinn asked.

"Whatever it takes to keep my little girl safe," he admitted.

"Then trust that you're the one this criminal wants to hurt," Quinn said. "Not her."

"Unless he realizes killing her is the worst way to hurt me."

A shiver ran down her spine even as she forced her

voice to sound confident. "We can't let ourselves think like that."

"I know you hate accepting help," Vic said, and Quinn realized for a moment she'd almost forgotten he was there. "But, bro, it's your brothers and sisters in the Canadian Rangers who are heading up this mission. They're military, like you, and that makes you family. Even if you've never met, they are willing to give their lives to protect your little girl."

Quinn watched as Jeff swallowed hard. The conversation turned to the practical matters of where the supposed ghost town was, how they'd keep in contact with Vic, and how they didn't have that much time until the rain was supposed to return and the treacherous storm was about to strike. They ended the call and walked down to the river together, where she blinked to see her very own canoe, paddle, life jacket and survival pack waiting for her.

"How did you know all this was my kit?" she asked.

"I didn't," he said and shrugged. "You and Addison were in danger and all that mattered was coming after both of you. So, I literally didn't stop to think, let alone figure out which canoe or life jacket would be yours. I just ran to the waterfront, grabbed what looked best, made a quick guess at what life jacket would fit you and jumped in. I'm fortunate that Marcel chased me down and forced his maps into my hand."

Quinn pressed her lips together and reached for her life jacket.

"You know, I hate admitting I need help and accepting it too," she said. She slid her life jacket on and buckled it up. It was damp and clammy on her skin, but she was beyond thankful to have it back. "I'm not letting you off the hook for being difficult when we worked together—"

Jeff threw the other life jacket on. "I wouldn't want you to—"

"But, as much as I say I wanted to work together," she said, "and learn from you, I also really like taking charge, being independent and doing things my way." That is why she loved the business and career she'd built so much. "So, we have that in common."

He pushed the canoe off the shore and into the water. "You're being too hard on yourself," he said.

"We have that in common too," she said. She climbed into the prow of the boat. Plus, neither of them coped well with being trapped in tight spaces. "You know, I always thought we didn't get along because we were opposites. But maybe it was because we had too much in common."

Jeff chuckled under his breath.

They set a course and hit the rapids. She sat in the bow and navigated, while Jeff sat in the stern and steered. For over an hour, neither of them said anything besides brief directionalities like "on your right" and "sharp left" as they paddled together like one seamless unit around the quick turns and jagged rocks that jutted dangerously out of the water, threatening to capsize and scuttle them at every turn.

The river branched into myriad side rivers and cut deep through granite. Sheer walls of rock rose high on either side. Fierce wind beat down on them, pushing them faster and faster. The sky grew darker, thunder rumbled like a warning in the distance, while the current grew ever more treacherous beneath their little canoe.

Her own thoughts and fears roiled within her. How long would Kelsey's attempts to keep everything as cheerful, upbeat and manufactured as something inside children's television screen last and the true terror of what was happening start to seep inside the little girl's heart? How long and how thoroughly had this been planned? And why had someone used her little wilderness tour company as a piece in the evil machinery they'd designed?

This route had been chosen from several Quinn had listed on her website and been voted on in a poll on her social media. Had Big Poppa engineered that? Bruno had only come on the trip because her initial guide had been in a hit-and-run car accident. Was Big Poppa behind that too? She now knew Bruno had been planted on her trip as part of this, and so had to assume her supposed accident at the falls might've been an attempt to either get her out of the way or cause a distraction. Trying to break into the cabin also might've been a distraction or a first attempt at kidnapping Addison. The truck crash could've also been a distraction or a way to get rid of Bruno after he'd failed Big Poppa or served his purpose.

Or multiple things could be true at once.

They were caught inside a web, ensnared on invisible threads that weaved all around them. With Big Poppa sitting like a fat and deadly spider in the middle, pulling the strings.

Lord, no matter how hard I try to cling to hope and faith, everything seems so hopeless. Please guide us.

Protect us. Bring Jeff's daughter back safely into his arms. End this nightmare.

Then, when she'd been paddling for so long her arms ached and her shoulders cried for mercy, the rain returned with a vengeance. Lightning flashed in the distance. The water grew choppier, splashing over the edges of their little boat while a deluge poured down on them from above.

"Keep paddling!" Jeff shouted. "I'll bail. We need to keep going."

"Will you pray with me?" she called back.

"Never been much for praying," he said. "Well, before today. But I'll give it a try."

"Lord, You promised that when we call out to You that You hear our cries," she shouted into the rain. "Please save us. Help us find Addison. Bring her home safely."

"And keep us from drowning," Jeff added.

"That too."

"Amen!" Jeff said. "Now, is my mind playing tricks on me or do you hear something flying toward us?"

"Flying?" she repeated. "In this storm?"

Suddenly she heard the staccato sound of what sounded like bullets exploding from a gun. The clatter of weapon fire echoed off the granite walls around them.

"Get down!" Jeff shouted. "We're under fire."

How and from where?

Bullets whizzed past her head and ricocheted off the rocks, sending debris and scrub showering around them. There was nowhere to run, let alone hide. Quinn bent as low as she could and sheltered her head in her hands.

"Help us, God!" Jeff shouted a prayer as bullets sprayed the water around them. "We're sitting ducks."

The bullets stopped. She searched through the rain for their attacker and finally saw what they were facing. A remotely controlled drone. The kind, she guessed, someone could buy for a whole lot of money from a very good aerial enthusiast's store. The kind someone had jerry-rigged into a deadly weapon by welding a semiautomatic to the bottom.

"It's a drone!" Quinn shouted. Where was the person operating it? There was nothing around here for miles. And yet, in one terrifying moment of clarity, everything made sense.

This could be how an unseen gunman had killed Bruno. How someone had blown up the cave and buried them inside. Why they'd heard and seen the approach of a dozen attackers in the woods when there'd just been two men. Someone was using a drone to terrify and terrorize them.

And now it was making a slow, sweeping turn, coming back their way.

"Jeff!" she shouted. "What do we do?"

She turned and looked at him over her shoulder. Something even more terrifying than the weaponized drone filled her eyes. Jeff was frozen. His face was pale, his eyes were wide, and his hands gripped his paddle so hard it was like he was about to snap it in two.

The drone began to fire. Bullets splashed through the water toward them. Fiberglass splinters and shards flew around her as weapon fire shredded part of the right side of the canoe. Whatever seeped through the bullet holes threatened to sink them. The drone flew past them, stopped and began to turn around again. Whoever was controlling the drone was doing so remotely and their aim was bad. The wind and the rain was no doubt making it much harder to both steer and aim.

But all it took was for one bullet to reach its mark.

Gingerly, Quinn placed her paddle in the middle of the canoe. Then she turned around in her seat, crouched low, and made her way toward Jeff. The canoe shook underneath her. She gritted her teeth and prayed they wouldn't tip. She reached Jeff and took his face in her hands.

"Jeff, listen to me," she said. Urgency and desperation coursed through her veins. "I need you right now, okay? Wherever you've disappeared to in your head, I need you to come back to me because I can't survive this without you."

Help me, Lord. I don't know what kind of trauma happened to him on the battlefield or the depth of pain it left inside him.

She took his face in her hands. "The drone and gunfire are real. We're together. We're in a canoe. We're being fired at and I need you."

His deep blue eyes snapped to her face. *"What do you need?"*

The drone was turning back toward them. Its red light blinked at them like an eye. It was a camera. Whoever was doing this to them was watching it happen.

They'd survived two passes. They wouldn't survive a third.

"Keep the boat steady," she said. "Whatever happens, don't let us flip."

They were going to need the canoe to get out of the river alive.

Carefully, she picked up her paddle and stood in the canoe, felt it rock unsteadily beneath her feet.

"Hey!" she shouted and waved at the drone. "Big Poppa! You want me? Well, here I am!"

The drone flew toward her like a hornet about to strike. She gripped the paddle tightly with both hands like a baseball bat, swung her arms around with precision aim and struck.

The paddle hit the drone with a crack that seemed to shake through her arms and reverberate in the air around them. The drone flew into the rock wall and smashed against the granite. A sudden burst of red flame flashed in front of her, blinding her gaze, before the drone dropped into the water below. Small trees and rock poured from the cliffside. The canoe shook wildly.

"Hang on!" Jeff shouted. "We're taking on water and it's thrown off the balance."

A jagged rock rose from the water ahead. Desperately, Quinn reached to try to steer them around it. But it was too late. They smashed against it. The canoe shook.

Quinn was tossed overboard.

Chaos engulfed Jeff's senses. The current spun him around in dizzying circles, making him feel like a Ping-Pong ball in the washing machine. The boat he sat in was sinking beneath him. The smell of gunfire still lingered in the air, despite the wind and rain that lashed against his body. They'd been attacked by a drone—just like the makeshift drone explosive that had killed Della and thirteen other members of his unit. That couldn't be a coincidence. Could it?

"Quinn!" he shouted. "Where are you?"

No answer. He gritted his teeth, wedged his paddle against a rock to stop the boat from spinning then leaned overboard and grabbed on to it. The rock was slippery against his fingers and he nearly lost his grasp. But he managed to lash a rope around it, anchoring the boat in place. The rock was narrow and incredibly uneven. He jammed his paddle between his seat and the side of the boat to keep it from floating away, looked around in vain for hers, and tucked the satellite phone and walkie-talkie into a pouch under the seat. Then he climbed out of the canoe onto the rock, balanced on it and scanned the water for Quinn.

A flash of bright yellow caught his eye in the distance. It was her life jacket.

He leaped into the water. Immediately the current swept him downstream from her. But he swam hard for the side of the river to where the granite cliff rose a story tall out of the water. He grabbed for the wall, lost his grip and was tossed farther downriver. He grabbed again and got a fingerhold. So far, so good. He gritted his teeth and forced his way along the wall toward Quinn, one step at a time, reaching for footholds under his feet and crawling his hands horizontally along the rock. Water beat against him, trying to force him back. His lungs and limbs ached with every step.

"Jeff!" Quinn's voice floated through the air toward him and he felt fresh air fill his lungs. "Help!"

"I'm coming!" he shouted back. "Are you okay?"

"Yes," she called. "But I'm trapped."

"Just hang on!" he told her. "I'm almost there." Rain beat against his head. His ankles and knees were bashed over and over again by unseen rocks under the water. "It's going to be okay. I promise!"

Then he saw Quinn pinned behind what looked like a fallen tree in a mass of rock and debris. Her eyes met his and a smile crossed his face.

"Hey," she said. "You made it."

"I did." The grin that he felt cross his face was exhausted and weak, but it was real. How was it that, no matter how much pain his heart and his body were in, she always managed to make him feel stronger than he knew he was capable of being? He wedged his feet between two rocks, grabbed on to the tree trunk. She reached her hand for his through the debris. He grabbed it and held on tightly.

"Are you okay?" he asked.

"Better than I was earlier today," she said. "My leg is snagged on something under the water and I can't get it free."

"Okay," he said. "Brace yourself on something solid if you can, because once I start pulling stuff loose, you might suddenly get washed downstream. Also, be sure to scream if I put pressure anywhere that hurts you."

"Will do," she said.

He gripped the tree trunk and leaned his full weight against it. Quinn wriggled her body backward. For a moment, he thought she'd made it, but then she stopped and shook her head.

"Hang on," he said. "I'll join you in there."

He crawled over the log until he was beside her. They bobbed side by side in the river.

"You've got quite the swing," he said. "Baseball?"

"That and hockey and lacrosse," she said. "I have a habit of getting penalties for high-sticking. I also won third place in a national junior girl's lumberjack championship when I was twelve. But that's swinging down not up."

"Well, it worked for you," he said. He started breaking off branches and tossing them downriver. Then his foot searched for hers in the water. He found it wedged under what felt like a tree root. Gently, he started kicking it free.

"How did all this end up in the water?" he asked.

"I think the drone exploded," she said. "Either it was set to detonate or whoever was flying it did so manually. Do you think that's how Big Poppa has done all of this? That he used drones with speakers to convince you that two kidnappers were twenty? That he used a drone equipped with an incendiary explosive to blow up the cave and another with a gun mounted on it to shoot Bruno?"

"Yeah, I do," Jeff said, grimly. It fit the facts plus it had the twisted bit of irony to it considering how Della and the others in his unit died.

"What I don't understand is how anyone is operating it out here," Quinn said. "There's nothing around for miles and I thought the flying range on these things wasn't that far."

"The range is a lot farther if it's a law enforcement or a military surveillance drone," he said. "In which case, the operator could be over an hour away as the crow flies, especially if he doesn't mind if it goes out of range because he wasn't planning on trying to fly it back."

Then the spark of a thought crossed his mind. If he got his hands on even part of the law enforcement drone, he might be able to use it to trace who Big Poppa was and put a stop to all of this. He gave another kick and Quinn yelped with happiness as she yanked her foot free.

"Thank you," she said. "Now it's time to get out of here, salvage whatever we can of the canoe. And figure out how we're going to make it to the ghost town."

He looked down at the churning green-gray water beneath them. Somewhere down there were the remains of the drone that had fired on them.

Jeff unzipped his life jacket.

"Now, you head downriver and try to save the canoe," he said. "It took some damage, but hopefully it'll float long enough to get us to where we need to be. I'm going to dive down to see if I can salvage anything from the drone."

"No, you're not," she said. "Your life is too important for me to let you risk it right now, diving into that current looking for drone parts."

"Quinn," he said wearily, "I get that you're worried. But you can't stop me."

"Oh, really?" She let go of her handholds on the fallen tree and grabbed the collar of his life jacket on both sides of the zipper as if trying to pull it closed. He felt her full weight tug against him, almost pulling him off the precarious footing he'd found.

His teeth clenched. "Let go."

"Not until you promise you're going to zip your life jacket back up and make your way to the canoe with me," she said.

He felt frustration building in the back of this throat. Was she serious with this? He couldn't remember the last time he let anyone tell him what to do, and even when he had been following orders from superior officers overseas, he hadn't always been a fan of it.

"Between the current and the storm, you're more likely to drown than find something," she said. "You know it as well as I do. And don't try to tell me that all you're going to do is make one quick dive and when if you find nothing, you'll give up. Because we both know that's not true and you'll keep risking your life going back over and over again."

"How could you possibly know that?" Jeff asked.

"Because that's what I'd do!" Her voice rose. "How about this? I'm every bit as strong a swimmer as you are, maybe even stronger. How about you stay up here and I take my life jacket off and I dive under and hunt for drone parts?"

"No." He didn't quite yell the word but it was so loud he heard it echo back to him against the rocks, blending with the noise of the rain and the wind. "I'm not going to let you risk drowning on a long shot!"

"Why?" she demanded. "Why is it okay for you to risk your life but not me?"

"Because I care about you!" he said.

More than he cared about himself.

"And I care about you," her voice dropped. "Despite everything that happened in the past, you're my friend, Jeff."

Yes, they were friends. And he'd never let himself hope for anything more. She deserved far better than to be saddled with a man like him.

"Friends don't let friends die, all right?" she added. Her luminous eyes searched his. "So I'm going to have your back. And you're going to have mine. Neither of us is going to risk our lives doing anything stupid. We're going to get through this together. Okay?"

He looked up at the sky and felt rain course down his face like tears.

"Somebody kidnapped my baby girl," he said. Sorrow wrenched through him like someone had thrust a hand inside his rib cage and twisted his heart. "If I don't keep throwing myself forward with every breath, I'm afraid I'll collapse."

"I know." Quinn's voice was soft. "But Addison doesn't need you to risk your life right now to solve the crime. Other people can do that. But you're the only person who can be her daddy. Addison needs you to find her, hold her in your arms and tell her that you love her. She doesn't need a detective right now. She needs you."

Hot tears pressed at the corners of his eyes and mingled with the cold raindrops.

"And I need you too, Jeff," Quinn's voice cracked and even though she didn't loosen her grip on his life jacket in the slightest, something about her touch felt more tender. "I need you to help me through today. I've never begged anyone for help in my life. But I'm exhausted, I'm sore, I'm terrified, and I'm overwhelmed. And I know you are as well. So, I need you, and I think you need me too, so we're going to get through this together."

He looked into her face and saw something floating in the depths of her eyes he'd never seen before. It was like caring but deeper than care. It was respect in a way that was tender. Compassion in a way that was fierce. It was a feeling he'd never before seen in any-one's eyes when they'd looked at him. Yet somehow he knew it was how he looked at her too. And while he had no hope of ever being worthy of being someone's husband, even if he was one day, he couldn't imagine finding someone as amazing as her.

"Okay," he said. His voice was so hoarse, the word was barely more than a gasp through his lips. He wasn't even sure she'd heard it until she let go of the life jacket, turned and swam toward the canoe, as if trusting im-plicitly he'd be true to his word.

He cast a long glance at the churning water around him, then zipped up his life jacket, climbed over the fallen tree and let the water carry him downriver toward her. He reached Quinn clinging to the same rock he'd anchored the boat to. The canoe, sunk to its gunwales, was almost completely submerged. Oh, no. Now what?

"I'm sorry," Jeff said.

"Don't worry," Quinn said. "You couldn't keep it from sinking."

"Which is exactly what I'd tell you if the roles were reversed," he said. "But you'd still blame yourself, right?" His paddle was still wedged in the canoe, but her paddle was long gone and he guessed she'd lost it when she'd demolished the drone and fallen overboard. He reached under the seat for the pouch. It was empty. His heart sank. "We've lost the satellite phone and the walkie-talkie."

Quinn shook her head. "We've lost Marcel's maps too. So we're paddling blind and with no way to contact the outside world." She shook her head and prayed. "Help us, Lord."

They half swam and half floated down the river, dragging the submerged canoe along with them by the rope. It was painful and treacherous going, and if it hadn't been for their combined strength and life jackets, they and the canoe wreckage would've been sucked under by the current multiple times.

Finally, the granite walls gave way to forest and they found an inlet and dragged themselves to shore, where they lay on the wet earth for a long moment, gasping for breath. Then they flipped the canoe over and did their best to drain it. Quinn fished some emergency duct tape strips from a pocket inside her life jacket and together they used it to patch the holes in the canoe the best they could. She found a piece of driftwood long and strong enough to be used as a paddle, and Jeff used his pocketknife to whittle it into a rough paddle shape.

Then they got back in the canoe and kept paddling. It was a slow and tedious journey. The rain continued to pound down on their heads, filling the boat and blinding their vision. No matter how hard and often he bailed, he could never rid the boat of the stubborn few inches of dirty water that sloshed around the bottom.

He watched Quinn's back as she paddled. After a while, her strong form faded and her shoulders began to sag. He paused paddling, leaned forward in the boat and brushed his hand her shoulder, feeling the tight knots of tension beneath his touch. She stopped paddling for a moment too, letting the very tip of the driftwood trail beside her in the water.

"Hey," he said. "Thank you for being here and putting yourself through all this for me and my daughter. I couldn't have done this without you."

"No problem," she said without turning.

But he felt the tension in her back relax under his touch. Then she straightened again and went back to paddling. So did he and they continued down the river in silence.

Darkness fell earlier than usual behind the heavy clouds. Rain continued to fall in steady, relentless sheets. Thunder rumbled closer. Forked lightning flashed in the distance above the trees, sending a jolt of fear through him. If the lightning grew closer, they'd have to pull over and find shelter. The safest place to be was inside right now and the second was in an open clearing away from the trees. But if the trees were dangerous at the moment, the water was an even more lethal superconductor for electricity. A lightning strike in the forest could be deadly under the best of circumstances, but if they were struck while out on the river, there'd be no coming back. He prayed the storm would stay at bay.

Jeff had no idea how long they'd been paddling when suddenly he heard Quinn gasp.

"Look!" she exclaimed.

He followed where her arm was pointing. Tall and shadowy shapes rose ahead of them through a break in the trees. He blinked. Was he seeing things? Or had they finally found the ghost town? Fresh hope rose in his chest. Had they finally found his little girl?

"I'm pulling over," Jeff said. He slowed the canoe and steered toward the shore.

A sudden roar sounded in the distance and, for a moment, he thought it was another rumble of thunder until he saw a shaft of light cut through the sheets of rain in front of him.

"It's a helicopter!" Quinn shouted. "Who'd be desperate enough to fly in a storm like this?"

Somebody looking for them. Or a ruthless criminal coming to collect a little girl he'd kidnapped?

The aircraft's beam swung through the darkness around him. It bounced off the dilapidated structure of a two-story mill complete with remains of an old wheel still spinning futilely in the wind. Then it turned and flew to the right, illuminating a smattering of cabins fading into the woods behind it. A small overgrown beach with posts where a dock had once stood was ahead on his right.

Well, it seemed they'd found what Marcel had told them to look for. And they weren't the only ones interested in it. He steered toward it. As they reached the shore, Quinn jumped out and pulled them aground. He leaped into knee-deep water and waded to the beach. Together they pulled the canoe up onto the shore.

"Why is it just hovering?" she asked.

"There's nowhere around here to land," he said. He looked at the canoe.

"Do you think they're here to rescue us?" Quinn asked.

"I don't know," he said. "It definitely looks like Canadian Rangers, but it's hard to tell in this storm." All he could do was hope. "If so, they'll have to either try to drop down a rope, which I wouldn't want to try climbing in this weather, or find a place to land somewhere else and hike to us."

But if this wasn't rescue, and instead how Big

Poppa had arranged to collect Addison from Kelsey and Benny, they were going to have a challenge getting her on the helicopter in this weather. And that would help buy Jeff and Quinn some time to find her.

A clap of thunder shook the air. Forked lightning spiked from the clouds and struck the helicopter with a metallic bang like something popping. It spun wildly and Jeff felt Quinn grab his hand and squeeze it tightly. Then the helicopter swerved sharply and disappeared over the trees.

Darkness fell across them again. Quinn let go of his hand, and Jeff realized his heart was pounding.

"Is the helicopter going to crash?" Quinn asked.

"If the pilot is a professional, probably not," he said. "But if they're an amateur or the lightning hit something vital—"

His words froze suddenly as the noise of the rotors and thunder faded and he heard another, plaintive sound filling in the darkness.

"Daddy! I want Daddy now!"

His knees buckled. He'd found his little girl. Addison was here. She was alive. And she was calling for him.

TEN

Addison! Jeff ran up the slope toward the shadowy structures of the ghost town. His ears strained to hear his little girl's voice. His heart beat like a drum in his chest, ready to battle a thousand foes to keep her safe. He reached an outcropping of small buildings, stopping at what he guessed had once been the entrance to the small town. Lightning flashed, illuminating the scene for an instant before it fell dark again. There were maybe ten wooden buildings, scattered and in various states of disrepair. He ran from building to building, bursting through doorways and breaking down doors. Empty rooms filled his eyes. She wasn't there. She wasn't anywhere. Was it another drone trick? She sounded so real and so close.

"No bed!" Addison's cries seemed to echo from all directions at once. "No more campin'! I want Gi'ant Dolly! I. Want. My. Daddy!"

Thunder roared like a lion. Desperation surged inside Jeff. It was like the instinct that had caused him to recklessly leap into the water to swim toward his brother's truck without stopping to check the current, only amped up to a thousand. He wanted to bellow his daughter's name into the night and tell her that her daddy was coming to save her. He wanted to pull out his knife and fight. Even as he could feel his brain telling him that he needed to take a breath, think and make a wise and cautious plan that wouldn't put anyone at unnecessary right, it was as if, in that moment, he didn't know how.

A memory he'd almost forgotten crossed his mind. He'd been sitting in the small, plain room they'd used for the brig when the unit's military chaplain had knocked on the door and asked to come in. For now, he couldn't remember the man's name, only that he was short, with gray hair and glasses, and had proved more than once that he could plank longer than anyone else on base. In hindsight, Jeff couldn't even remember what the man had actually said to spark a reaction. All he remembered was standing there in front of this placid man twice his age and saying, "I like who I am. I like that I stand up to bullies and don't let people get hurt on my watch. And I'm not going to let them change me."

The military chaplain had crossed his arms. "Jeff, I don't want to change you. I want you to learn to harness all that. You ever seen water cascading violently over a hydro dam powering a city? Giving life to schools, hospitals and families? You see ever a turbine moving in the wind? Take everything in you—your heart, your drive, your fight, your power—and use it to change the world instead of destroying yourself."

Jeff blinked back the memory and realized he'd run off without the one person who'd come on this journey with him and had the most inside knowledge on the kidnappers. He turned to walk back to Quinn and saw her already standing a few steps behind him.

"I can't find her," he said. "She's not here. I feel like I'm drowning in blinding panic and rage, and that scares me."

And right now that fear was paralyzing him. Quinn walked to him until they were in the middle of the clearing. Thunder and lightning crashed again in unison, illuminating her face as they stood there in the center of the storm.

"Quinn, why do I feel like my mind is blank and I've got lava in my veins?" he said. "I'm better than this. I'm a military veteran. I'm a Canadian Ranger. Rescuing people is my living."

"You're also a father," she said, "whose little girl is crying." She reached out, grabbed his hand and pressed it against the curve of her neck. Her pulse raced. "Feel that?" she asked. She dropped his hand. "I feel ready to pass out and had to take a few deep breaths before I ran up here. I've never been a parent, but I've had a father who I loved more than anything in the world. And I would quite literally give up my own life and die for your kid."

"No camp'in!" Addison's voice seemed to come from every direction at once. "Want my bed! Want Daddy!"

"Jeff." Urgency filled Quinn's voice as she fixed her eyes on him. "You know Addison better than anyone else in this world. Why is she crying right now?"

"What do you mean why?"

"Focus," Quinn said. "Is she hurt? Is she scared for her life?"

"She's angry and defiant," he said. "She gets like

this at bedtime. She won't sleep without her Giant Dolly and bedtime stories. Plus, it's still well over an hour too early before bedtime. Someone is trying to tell her to go to sleep and she's not having it."

Relief brushed his shoulders. Already he could tell her voice was coming from a wooded area to the right of them.

"And I think it's really her," he added. "After everything, I can't discount the fact it's a drone. But Addison's got a strong set of lungs and really wails when she's being stubborn. That little girl's voice gets so high-pitched, she could almost break glass. No way someone could project that through a speaker without at least some distortion."

They unzipped their life jackets, left the buildings and moved through the trees toward the sound of Addison's voice. Nothing but darkness and trees filled his gaze. He listened as Addison's voice settled down and fell silent, only to surge again moments later in a fresh burst of defiance. No this couldn't be another drone trick like the one played on them back at camp. Her voice sounded too alive, close and above all real.

He'd never been so thankful for having a little girl who was cranky when it came to an unwanted bedtime. Then he saw the faint light trickling through the trees. He followed it like a beacon through the storm. There stood a small wooden cabin, slightly larger than the others, with both a front and back window. Quinn's hand brushed his arm as if to silently tell him that she'd seen it too. A yellow beam emanated from the front window, which he guessed by the angle was a flashlight. But the back window was still dark. Did that mean the cabin had two rooms?

They crept closer. Three voices came into focus now. Benny was frustrated, swearing at Kelsey and complaining that Big Poppa was late. Whether or not that had actually been Big Poppa in that helicopter, which he guessed by their arguing they hadn't actually seen, Benny was convinced Big Poppa would be picking them up, somehow, at any moment to take them out of there. And for some reason Benny had been unable to reach him by satellite phone for over an hour. Meanwhile, Kelsey was trying to coax Addison to lie down on a sleeping bag with an odd, childlike singsong voice that seemed to be fraying with fatigue and stress at the edges. Addison was loudly and stubbornly refusing to sleep.

Jeff and Quinn reached the house and sat on the ground against the side.

"You wait here," he whispered. "I'll check around back."

She nodded.

He gestured to her to stay put and made his way around to the back. The window was a shadowed empty gap in the wall where glass had once been. He glanced in, saw nothing but bare floor illuminated by dim light seeping through from the doorway to the other room. He took off his life jacket, eased his body through headfirst, hit the soft, wet planks, and rolled without making a sound. He found himself in a small and dark room, and crouched up on the balls of his feet and listened. Through the gaps in the dilapidated wall, he could catch of glimpse of what was happening in the other room.

The room was long and at least three times the length of the one he was in now. Wind whistled through the chinks in the walls. Missing floorboards punctuated the room like keys in a broken piano.

Then he saw Addison, sitting so close to him now that if he just reached his fingers through the gaps in the planks he'd have been able to touch her golden hair. Benny paced in and out of frame, stepping from one floorboard to another, clutching a gun in one hand, a satellite phone in the other. Dangerous tension radiated through the young man's frame and Jeff was suddenly reminded of the expression that an addict in painkiller withdrawal would "kill" for a fix. His heart ached and, although he knew he should climb back outside, something inside him was desperate to stay. Then he heard an eager yip and the sound of paws skittering across the floor. He saw Butterscotch charging toward the darkened doorway.

Jeff rushed to the window, dove out headfirst into the bushes and lay there not daring to risk moving or making a sound in case the dog gave up his location.

"Bu'er'scotch come here!" Addison yelled. "No run!"

The dog's footsteps clattered back into the other room. Jeff let out a long breath. He crawled back to where Quinn sat against the wall beneath the glow of a light-filled window. He sat alongside her, underneath the shelter of the sloping roof and out of the rain. He leaned his head close to hers.

"That was close," he said and told her what he'd seen through the gaps in the wall. "I thought for a moment the dog was going to blow my cover."

"Me too," she whispered. "I risked a glimpse through

window. Same as you, I've got Benny guarding the front door. He's jittery, and the only person who's armed. But he is also holding the phone, which will slow his reaction time."

"Did you see where Addison and Kelsey were?" he asked. "I could only see the back of Addison's head."

"They're sitting on a sleeping bag against the back wall," she said.

"How far from the door to the other room?" Jeff asked.

"Not even six feet," Quinn said. "All it would take is a distraction at the front door to draw Benny and Kelsey's attention away from Addison, and you could slip in from the room and grab her."

That meant Quinn would be the one drawing the kidnappers toward her.

"I agree our top priority is getting Addison away from them," he said. "We don't want to risk her getting caught in the line of fire if Benny pulls the trigger. But I don't exactly like the idea of you getting a man with a gun to chase you through the trees."

"Neither do I," Quinn said. "But it has to be you that rescues her. She loves and trusts you without hesitation. If anything goes wrong, you need to be the one getting her to safety."

His daughter's wailing grew louder, demanding a snack, a drink, all her favorite toys and her bed at home. She was headed for a full-on tantrum now. Kelsey's cajoling was starting to sound panicked. Benny was yelling and swearing, as if trying match Addison for volume.

They had to get Addison out of there before Benny snapped.

"It's going to be okay," Quinn said. "Just run around to the back and get your little girl. Trust me. Even if I can only pull Benny away, I've never seen Kelsey with a weapon or show any aggression. I'm confident you'll be able to take Addison from her."

But just because that had been true of Kelsey didn't mean she couldn't snap as well.

"He'll kill you," Jeff said. *And I don't think I'm ready to live without you.*

"No, he might try to kill me," Quinn said. "He might just kidnap me again. Either way, he'll have to try to catch me first. Addison will be safer if you are the one snatching her from danger. You're physically stronger, you can carry her better than I can, and she trusts you. And you know it."

She was right and he knew it. But he also didn't like it.

"Plus, I've tangled with Benny before," she added. "I know how to get under his skin."

He really did not like the sound of that.

"Is there anything I can say to change your mind?" he asked.

"No." She reached over and wrapped her arms around him in a sideways hug. He felt her lips brush against the rough line of his jaw. He slid his arms around her, pulled her close and breathed her in.

"You stay safe, okay?" Jeff asked. "I'm not leaving these woods without you."

"I'll be fine," she said. "Just go."

Somehow her words weren't as reassuring as his

heart needed them to be. As Quinn turned and, without looking back, made her way around to the front of the cabin, he realized he'd never asked her what her plan for a diversion to pull Benny and his gun away from Addison was going to be. He crawled around to the back window, checked the room was empty and once again slid his body into the dark room.

Then he waited, crouched just inches away from his daughter, listening to the arguing and tension still erupting in the other room, his heart aching for the moment he could pull Addison safely into his arms.

Moments ticked by. It might not have been more than a few seconds, each one seemed to stretch out to fill an eternity.

Lord, I don't know if You're listening, but I promise You that if You bring me safely out of this with my daughter, I will do everything in my power to be the best father I can be and give her the life and happiness she deserves.

Knocking sounded hard and purposeful on the cabin's front door. Kelsey and Benny fell silent as their heads turned toward the sound. Butterscotch barked and ran for the door so quickly his feet slid on the wood floor. The rapping continued, Benny crossed the floor and Jeff's heart began to sink.

No... It couldn't be...

Benny slid the phone into his pocket, checked the clip of his gun for bullets, and yanked the door open.

There stood Quinn on the doorstep. And like a bolt of lightning through his heart, Jeff realized why Quinn hadn't told him what her plan and the distraction was going to be that would allow him to grab his little girl and take her to safety.

It was Quinn. She was the diversion and she was putting her life directly on the line to help him save his daughter.

Quinn watched as all the color drained from Benny's face as if he were staring into the eyes of a ghost. The gun shook in his hand. And for the first time since the day had begun, Quinn genuinely wondered what she actually looked like at the moment. She'd nearly drowned, been drugged, dragged across the ground and buried alive, and then crawled her way out again. Jeff had never once said anything to make her feel self-conscious enough to think about her clothes, face or hair. But now, as she watched the abject horror cross Benny's face, she wondered just how dirty and bedraggled she must be. His eyes widened like he didn't know whether to scream, attack her or pass out. She glanced past him to his sister Kelsey. The young woman definitely looked like she was ready to faint. They'd also both turned away from Addison.

"You're…you're…" Benny repeated the word like he had no idea which one came next. "I…I…"

"I'm alive," she said in a low and harsh tone she hoped was soft enough Addison wouldn't hear. Butterscotch the puppy circled Quinn's feet and sniffed. The little girl's fussing had stopped so suddenly it was as if an unseen someone had signaled to her to shush. "After you drugged me, dragged me to a cave and buried me alive."

Benny's mouth opened and closed again. Anger

pooled into the edges of his eyes. But the only word he managed to bluster was, "How?"

"How did I dig myself out?" she asked. "Slowly, rock by rock."

And with the help of the most incredible man I've ever met, who right now is hiding behind the wall at the back of this room waiting to rescue his daughter from your clutches.

She looked past him to Kelsey, who was shaking so hard she looked sick. And Addison, who was sitting on the floor, with a puzzled look in her eyes as her tears dried, as if listening to a sound only she could hear. And past her, through the knots in the well-worn wood on the floor, she saw a silhouette move and heard the faintest creak of a footstep on the floorboards. It was Jeff. He was there waiting, watching, and biding his time until he was ready to strike.

Fresh courage surrounded Quinn like a cloak.

Benny waved the gun at her. "Get in the cabin."

No. No matter what, that wasn't going to happen. His gaze was more than cold and angry now. It was desperate, or even panicked, like a cornered animal. She'd been wrong about him earlier. While Kelsey might want to keep Addison alive, Benny was angry enough to snap. She still believed he'd never fired a gun at someone before. But as Quinn planted her feet on the front doorstep, feeling the storm rain down around her like a curtain, she knew that if she stepped foot inside the cabin and let him close the door behind her, there was no way she'd be making it out alive.

The puppy scampered away from Quinn and darted

across the floor to Addison. She watched as the little girl scooped the dog up into her arms.

"I don't want to fight with you," Quinn said, deciding to level the truth as a strategic weapon. "I saw a helicopter circling outside like it was looking for someone. I wondered if that was your ride coming to pick you up and if you had any way to call or signal them. I've had enough of this forest and I'm willing to call a truce if it gets us all home."

If it gets Addison home safely to her real home with her daddy who loves her.

"Kelsey!" Benny called. He tossed the satellite phone to his sister so quickly she fumbled as she caught it. "Get out there, find that helicopter and keep calling Big Poppa until he answers."

"I'm not leaving Addison," Kelsey said and her head shook. "I'm taking her with me. I'm not leaving her with you."

"I'm done doing it your way!" Benny shouted. "Thirty thousand dollars for the little girl alive and happy, you said. But only ten thousand if she's dead. So what? Who cares? It wasn't supposed to be like this. It wasn't supposed to take this long. And I'd rather take my share of ten and run. I'm done digging my way deeper into this!"

Kelsey ran past him and into the darkness.

Urgently, Quinn's eyes darted to Addison, praying she hadn't heard those terrible words. But the little girl and her puppy were gone. Emptiness filled the place where the child had once sat. Prayers of thanksgiving to God burst like fireworks through her core and she knew without a doubt that Addison was with Jeff.

Lightning flashed across the sky outside for a brief moment, and there, in the back room doorway, she saw Addison tucked safely and securely within the shelter of her father's arms. Jeff bent his head protectively over his daughter. He glanced up and his blue eyes met Quinn's for one silent and searing moment that seemed to shake something inside her she couldn't put into words. Then he turned toward the window and climbed out.

Benny swiveled. "What are you looking at?" His gun spun wildly around the cabin. "Where's the girl? Where'd she go?" He started for the back door. She couldn't let him find them. "Look, kid, if you're hiding, you'd better come out if you know what's good for you—"

Quinn punched Benny in the back of the head as hard as she could with the strongest right hook she could muster. He swore and dropped the gun. It clattered to the floor and spun, sliding into a gap between the missing floorboards. Then he turned on her. Vile swear words dripped like poison from his lips as venom filled his eyes. A knife flicked open in his hand. "I'm going to kill you for that."

He lunged at her and she ran, leaping through the open door and pelting out into the night. She ran blind and pushed her way into the trees, knowing with every step she was leading Benny farther and farther from Jeff and his daughter, giving them time to get away and escape. Jeff had rescued Addison. She was safe in his arms. All they had to do now was find somewhere to hide until his brother Vic and the Canadian Rangers came to their rescue. And while she prayed she'd be alive to see it, she knew that if she didn't make it, Jeff and his daughter would be worth giving her life for.

She felt Benny's knife catch the shoulder of her life jacket and slash deep into the fabric. She yanked free, feeling a chunk of the compact foam tear loose. And, for a terrifying moment, she nearly fell. He grabbed her by the shoulder. She tossed him off hard and he fell to the ground. She kept running.

Lord, I don't know where I'm going or what the end game is. Please help me. Please guide me. And no matter what happens to me, keep Jeff and Addison safe.

Something rustled in the trees ahead of her. A figure loomed in the darkness. The silhouette of a tall man with broad shoulders was striding toward her. Who was he? What did he want?

Quinn stifled a scream and turned so sharply she nearly lost her footing. Now she was headed toward the water. There was no way out. She'd have to try to make it to the canoe. And if she couldn't, she'd have to leap into the pitch-black waters and swim for it. The sound of Benny behind her grew closer. Other indistinct voices were shouting in the trees. They weren't alone. There was someone else there chasing her in the darkness. She was surrounded.

The ground sloped steeply beneath her. She stumbled down an incline. Benny leaped and caught her around the knees like a football tackle. She tumbled to the ground, feeling him on top of her. They rolled down the hill. Her head cracked against a rock and dizziness overwhelmed her. She felt Benny rise over her then bend down. The prick of a knife pressed slowly into the soft skin at the center of her neck. He snarled, "This ends now."

She kicked up desperately and knocked him back. He lunged forward again. The knife flashed. Suddenly a figure charged from the darkness with a barely restrained roar. He grabbed Benny by the scruff of the neck, yanked him off Quinn and pressed him to the ground, pinning him there and wrenching the knife from his hand. Benny swore violently, futilely threatening all kinds of revenge she could tell by his tone he wouldn't be able to affect.

"Jeff?" she called. She scrambled to her feet. "Is that you?"

"Yeah, it's me." His voice moved warm and protectively in the darkness. "I'm here. I've got you." But what was he doing there? Where was Addison? "Just give me a second to tie this guy's hands and stop his noise. And then I'll explain everything."

Benny's verbal assault was muffled. Yet he still made enough of a racket she could tell Jeff had gagged him with cloth and far more kindly than Benny had gagged her.

A distant light swung through the forest to her right, illuminating the scene. She blinked into the light but couldn't see who was behind the beam. Benny was on the ground with his hands tied behind his back and gagged with a bandana. Jeff stood over him. He turned and fixed his gaze on her. His hands reached out. Exhaustion and relief seemed to pour over his strong form. "Thank you," he said. "You…" His voice caught in his throat before their hands could meet and his lips could say another word.

"Daddy!" Addison's voice chirped through the trees. "You found Quinn!"

He chuckled. "Yes, Little Girl, I did."

Then she saw Jeff's brother step out of the trees, backlit by another still distant rescue person, who was holding the flashlight and now seemed to be running toward them. Vic cradled a squirming Addison in one arm and an equally rambunctious puppy in the other.

Addison practically lunged out of her uncle's grasp toward her father.

"Here," Jeff said to Vic and opened his arms. "Let me take her. You can take over this guy." He gestured to Benny. "I recommend finding a dry corner in one of the houses in the main circle to put him in. Somewhere we can keep an eye on him."

Vic set the dog down by Jeff's feet and strode over to where Benny lay on the ground. But Quinn's ability to focus on the brothers' conversation faded as the person with the flashlight came closer and she realized it wasn't some Canadian Ranger or law enforcement stranger. It was Rose. A sob escaped Quinn's lips and was echoed by her sister. They threw themselves into each other's arms and hugged, laughing and crying together in relief.

"I'm sorry I'm late to the party," Rose said when the sisters finally pulled away. "Jeff told us that Benny had lost his gun in the floorboards of the house. So I went, found it and secured it. But I didn't see any sign of the female kidnapper."

So, Kelsey was still out there somewhere in the darkness, with a satellite phone, trying to reach Big Poppa. At least, as far as they knew, she wasn't armed.

"What are you doing here?" Quinn asked.

"Vic came back to the house to help with the evacuation of your campers," her sister said. "As I think you've heard, a friend of a friend of Leia's fiancé had space for them at a place only three hours away from the cabin. They were reunited with their luggage and belongings there. Then I hitched a ride on the helicopter with Vic, coming to look for you."

"Which I objected to," Vic cut in. "And only gave in because you promised to follow direction."

Vic reached into his pocket, pulled out a second flashlight and switched it on. Then he hauled Benny to his feet with his other hand and steered him toward the ghost town.

"We saw you from the helicopter in the canoe but then we were struck by lightning," Rose said. "It was a pretty loud and scary moment. I won't lie. But the pilot was amazing. And managed to find a safe place to lower Vic and me down by rope."

"If I remember correctly—" Vic stopped walking and turned back "—I told you to stay in the helicopter and let me go down alone."

Was it her imagination or did her sister actually blush?

"Well…yeah, you did," Rose said. "But there were two harnesses, and I didn't think you'd meant it."

"I meant it!" Vic called. His voice was almost indignant. He resumed walking Benny back to town.

Jeff laughed. "Guess I should've warned you, bro," Jeff shouted after him. "The Dukes sisters are some of the toughest, bravest people in this world."

"I'll give you guys a moment," Rose said. "Also I'm

going to use Vic's satellite phone to call the family and let them know you're okay. Sounds like Leia and Sally have got everyone we've ever met camped out at the farmhouse overnight."

"Tell them I'll call them in a minute," Quinn said.

"Will do." Rose set the flashlight down against a rock so the beam of light illuminated Jeff and Quinn. Then she turned and followed after Vic and Benny.

"Quinn!" Addison reached out both arms within her daddy's grasp. "Want hug."

"Definitely."

Quinn turned toward the little girl and opened her arms, expecting Jeff to pass her to her. Instead, Jeff stepped forward, slid one arm around Quinn's waist and pulled her in. Quinn put one arm around the little girl and the other around her father. Addison wrapped her little arms tightly around Quinn's neck. The three of them stayed there for a long moment, holding each other. And when she tried to pull away, Addison clutched her tighter and tucked her head against her. So she stayed there, with her arms around Jeff and Addison, and their arms around her, feeling relieved, happy and whole in way she couldn't explain and had never felt before. Until finally the little girl broke the hug first.

"Done hug now, Daddy," she said firmly. "Put me down."

"Okay." Jeff pulled away slowly and set her down.

Quinn stepped back and picked up the flashlight. Addison slid one small hand into Quinn's and took her father's hand with the other. They started back for the cabin slowly, with Addison walking between them and the dog scampering ahead through the trees. It was only then she realized the rain had stopped to a faint drizzle.

"When do we get out of here?" she asked.

"As soon as they're able to send another rescue helicopter out here," Jeff said, "which won't be until they're positive the storm isn't about to surge back, considering the last one was struck by lightning."

"But we've now got a way to contact the outside world?" she asked.

"We do," Jeff said. She watched as worry lines creased his brow. "We're definitely better off than we were. But they're no closer to figuring out who Big Poppa is, still haven't managed to bring Paul in for questioning, and got nothing useful so far out of talking to Pastor Drew and his wife. And while I'm beyond thankful we're all together and finally have backup, for now we're still stuck in the woods—just the five of us with no way out."

"Plus we now have a hostage," Quinn said, "which complicates things. And Kelsey's out there somewhere in the night with a phone, able to contact Big Poppa and tell him where we are."

Big Poppa was still on his way, and when he arrived, they'd have no choice but to fight and no way to escape him.

ELEVEN

About an hour later, Quinn and Jeff were sitting side by side in the doorway of one of the abandoned cabins in the center of the ghost town, looking out at the starless night. The treacherous rain had stopped for now and heavy clouds hung across the sky, blocking out the stars. She could hear the gentle sound of Addison's breath rising and falling as she slept peacefully on the sleeping bag in the empty room behind them and the wheezing snores of the puppy sleeping alongside her.

Two flashlight beams moved periodically through the darkness at different ends of the ghost town as Rose and Vic patrolled the area. Quinn had called the family farmhouse and assured her sisters Leia and Sally that she was alive and well, after Jeff had used the phone to notify the police about Benny. Law enforcement had assured him the police would accompany the rescue efforts to arrest Benny. In the meantime, Vic had done his best to make sure Benny had a fairly comfortable and dry cabin to wait in on the opposite side of the town square. There'd been no sign of Big Poppa yet, and Kelsey seemed to have disappeared into the night.

In the meantime, all they could do was patrol and wait.

Silently, she turned and looked at Jeff in the darkness. He was staring straight ahead into the trees. They'd set another flashlight Vic had brought by their feet in the dirt and angled it slightly upward against a rock, so it would give them some light without shining directly on Addison. Quinn watched as its beam sent shadows flickering along his jawline and up the side of his face.

Addison had been exhausted by the time they'd gotten back to the cabins. Thankfully, Vic had brought with him an emergency pack that had included blankets, so they'd been able to make her a soft, fresh bed to sleep on, away from the cabin Benny and Kelsey had held her in. Both Jeff and Quinn had curled up on opposites sides of Addison on the floor, creating a protective shell around her and holding her hands as she finally settled down. Then Quinn and Jeff had taken turns telling her stories, singing her songs, and praying with her until the little girl's eyes had finally closed, her breaths had slowed and she'd fallen asleep. Even then they'd stayed there, on opposite sides of her, with her small hands in theirs, until she'd pulled away in her sleep, curled up into a ball and wrapped her arms around Butterscotch as he nuzzled into her neck. She'd buried her face in his fur.

Only then did Quinn and Jeff give up their posts at her side, creep to the doorway and sit there, silently looking out at the night.

For a long time, neither of them spoke. Quinn brushed her shoulder against Jeff's and as she was about to pull away, he leaned into her, nudging her head onto his shoulder. Gently, their fingers touched and then they linked, and she felt his thumb brush the side of her hand.

She closed her eyes. She'd had no idea that peace could somehow coexist alongside fear or that in the middle of a terrifying ordeal it was still possible to feel safe. When her sister Leia had fallen in love with her detective fiancé, Jay, they'd uncovered the truth about the killer who'd caused their father to hide her and her sisters away from the world and train them to protect themselves from evil. But looking back, she knew without a doubt that she'd had a happy childhood filled to the absolute brim with joy and love. She prayed as she sat there, that no matter what happened next, God would provide the same for Addison.

"Do you think she'll remember any of this?" Jeff whispered in the darkness, as if reading her mind.

"Probably not," Quinn said. She turned and looked at him. "I was around her age when my mother died, and I don't remember much of anything about it, except for the flowers when my father took us to lay bouquets on her grave."

He sighed. "What do I do if she remembers?"

"You help her reframe the stories," she said. "You give her new context, focus on the parts about love and courage, and not on the darkness and fear. You heard how hard Kelsey worked to keep Addison from being afraid. I think she'll be confused. And if she needs professional help, you'll be there to help her find it. My sister's fiancé says more than one of the people in his trauma group have gotten family counseling with their kids."

She caught herself and stopped, remembering how negatively Jeff had reacted before when she'd mentioned therapy and how hard he'd insisted that he was fine and didn't need therapy. And even while she was pretty sure she'd watched him freeze with panic during the drone strike on the river, she also wasn't about to try to pry his heart open to talk about anything he wasn't yet ready to deal with.

But something must've shown on her face because he squeezed her hand gently.

"What is it?" he asked.

"I don't want to overstep and pry into things that aren't any of my business," she admitted.

"Thank you," he said. He leaned toward her and rested his head on top of hers. "But I think you being here, and going through everything we went through, makes you part of this and I owe you some answers to your questions earlier."

"You really don't..." she started.

"Well, I want to." He pulled away and then turned to look at her on the step. His knees bumped against hers. "I never answered your question about how Addison's mother died because I blame myself for her death."

The words were so simple and straightforward, yet they seemed to shake the air around them harder than any roaring current or thundering storm ever could.

"I'm afraid I'll never forgive myself for that," he added, "and carrying that guilt forever is going to ruin my life, my ability to be Addison's father, and every relationship I'll ever have."

She searched his face, willing her mind to find the right words to say but failing. His eyes met hers, like a man who was drowning and needed someone to throw him a lifeline to help him swim his way to shore. She lifted her hand to his face and cradled his jaw against her palm. He closed his eyes for a long moment, and she watched as his breathing slowed.

"Fourteen members of my unit, including Della, died when insurgents attacked their convoy a few months before I met you while I was serving overseas," he said.

She took her hand away. He opened his eyes. She expected him to pull away but instead he took both of her hands in his and held them tightly.

"I'm sorry," she said. "I can't even imagine. Do you want to talk about it?"

"I was supposed to be leading a convoy between a base and a remote outpost," he said. "Navigation is one of my specialties. But instead of doing my job that day, I was sitting in the brig. Because the day before I'd seen a senior officer bullying a new recruit, so I jumped in between them and confronted him. I know I raised my voice and used language I shouldn't have. A couple of witnesses said I might've pushed him, not that I remember doing it. In the end, I wasn't even disciplined beyond a day in the brig and a reminder to be thankful it wasn't going on my record."

He blew out a long, hard breath.

"At the time, it all seemed so unfair," he said. "Now, in retrospect, they might've treated me better than I deserved. But the bottom line is that I should've been leading that convoy, and instead a less experienced soldier was, and they were struck by a makeshift drone with explosives attached."

She gasped a painful breath. "So that's why you froze when we were attacked by a drone," she said.

"Yeah." He nodded. "And I can't shake the feeling that it's personal. That's why I'm convinced that once they find Della's former fiancé, Paul, they'll prove he's Big Poppa. Because the fact he's using drones and Della was killed by a drone can't be a coincidence."

"You said something about him stirring up anger online," she said. "There are thirteen other people who lost family members in that attack. Maybe one of them is Big Poppa instead. Either way, I'm sure law enforcement is looking into it."

"I can't shake it," Jeff said. "It's like the memories of surveying the bombed out remains of the vehicles after I got out of the brig are always there, right under the surface, ready to emerge when I'm least expecting them. I can see it, smell it, and feel it on my skin. It makes me feel like I'm permanently broken."

She pulled her hands from his and wrapped them around him. She hugged him tightly and he clutched her, as if somehow they could hold each other's broken pieces together.

"You've got to know you can't blame yourself for that attack," she said. "If you'd been there, you might not have seen it. You might've died in the explosion. If you had seen the drone and it had been shot down by a fellow soldier, someone might've used another drone to attack another convoy or another day when you weren't there."

"I know," he said. "That's what Vic keeps trying to tell me." He lowered his voice, like he was mimicking his brother. "'Survivors guilt isn't logical,' he says.

'You've gotta see it's a lie'. But it's easier to say than believe. Or maybe it's easier to beat myself up for not stopping it than acknowledging I couldn't. But that's why I didn't press charges against Paul for threatening me because I thought I deserved it."

She pulled back from the hug and looked into the dark depths of his blue eyes.

"Because you think that if you'd been a good person then Della would've loved you, wanted to marry you and treated you better?" She hazarded a guess. "You blame yourself for how she treated you. She hurt you badly, and instead of blaming her, it made you hate yourself?"

"Maybe," he said. "I do know that I wasn't driven by genuine caring as much as the fact I wanted so badly to prove to her that was wrong about me. I'd never failed so epically at something before or had someone treat me like that. Something inside me wanted to fight to prove myself and win her over. Instead of just being willing to walk away from her hate.

"To be honest, I don't even think I wanted her in my life, let alone as a partner, even though I was willing to marry her for the sake of Addison. Then, when she died, all I could think was that I'd somehow proved I was every bit as worthless as she'd said I was, by not being there to save her." He stood and walked three paces away into the night before stopping and turning back. "I can't believe I just admitted that. Do you think I'm irrational?"

"I think the way she treated you had nothing to do with you and everything to do with her own broken-ness," Quinn said. "Like she was carrying her pain about her father through life and projecting it onto you. I think it's good you know that the fact you wanted to win her over doesn't mean it was a genuine romance. Look, if I'm honest, a really big part of me blames myself for the fact Bruno's dead and the fact Addison was kidnapped, and I'm terrified that everyone else will blame me for that too—"

"Seriously?" Jeff blinked. "You can't blame yourself for that. None of what happened today was your fault."

"So, you don't blame me at all for the fact Big Poppa somehow infiltrated my business, trip and campers in order to terrorize you and kidnap your little girl?" she asked, rising. "Or for not finding a way of staying with her instead of being buried in that cave. Because you could. And the campers and their families might blame me for the ordeal I put them through today. Why did Big Poppa choose me, my company, and my trip? Is it because he thought I was naïve, weak or easy to manipulate? Why was Bruno, a man I've worked with on multiple trips before, willing to betray me that way? What if I could have somehow seen it and stopped it? What if I could've done more? And Addison grows up to blame me?"

Thunder rumbled softly in the distance. Electricity seemed to crackle in the air between them and, for a long moment, neither of them said anything.

"You do sound a lot like me," Jeff said finally.

"I told you we were more alike than I'd realized," she said. She took a deep breath. Okay, if he'd opened up and been honest, she could too. "There's also something I haven't told you about me. My business is struggling financially. I'm barely getting by and I was counting on the positive buzz from this one trip to give me the boost I needed to salvage my dream and keep my business alive. Now, after all this, I can't imagine anyone will ever be willing to trust their lives to traveling with me ever again. And I'm worried the fact I was so focused on saving my business made me more vulnerable to Big Poppa or meant I missed something crucial that could've stopped all this from happening."

"You know I could never—will never—blame you for anything that happened today," Jeff said. "None of this is your fault. You can't take any of this on. As far as I'm concerned, you saved my daughter's life—at least twice, maybe more—and I will always be in your debt over that."

"Why can't you feel the same way about yourself the way you feel about me?" she asked.

"Quinn…" He chuckled softly. "I've never liked anyone, including myself, anywhere near as much as I like you."

He meant as a friend, right? Because she was pretty sure that he wasn't looking for a romantic relationship. Neither was she. And either way she couldn't start something with a man who wasn't ready to be there for her.

Still, something tightened in her chest and she stepped toward him in the dark and he met her halfway. His hands cupped her elbows and her hands brushed his forearms. Then he leaned forward and rested his forehead against hers. "You're one of the most caring, gutsy, strongest people I've ever known. I wish I was more like you."

She pulled her head back just enough that she could look up into his eyes.

"Are you kidding?" She felt her voice rise with sincerity. "You're incredible. You're selfless and courageous. Not to mention really sweet and funny. The way you love your daughter is so powerful, and I'm inspired by the way you'd give everything for her. You're the kind of man anyone would want as a father." She broke his gaze and looked down at their feet. "Or a husband. You have no idea how many of our old campers pointed out how good looking you were and told me they were going to ask you out."

"A lot of them did," he said. "But I never said yes. Then I found out a lot of people thought I was all hung up on you,"

"What?" An unexpected laugh burst through her lips. Her hands slid onto his shoulders. "Really?"

"Yeah," he said. "People thought I had a crush on you."

"But you didn't," she said. "Obviously."

"Maybe I did," he said, "and just wasn't ready to admit it to myself."

"Well, maybe I used to have a crush on you," she said. Even though *crush* felt like such a frivolous word to describe the mixture of admiration, emotional connection and respect she felt inside her.

But it was all in the past, right? Because neither of them wanted a relationship. And even if they did, she had to worry about her business and he had to focus on Addison. Their lives were heading in different directions.

His eyes widened. "No one's told me they had a crush on me before."

His arms slid around her waist and enveloped her. She slid her hands around his neck and pulled him closer to her. Her face rose to meet his as he bent toward her. And suddenly, unexpectedly and sweetly, their lips met.

For a long, gentle moment, she kissed him and was kissed by him, feeling safe and at peace, comfortable in a man's embrace in a way she never had before.

"Good news about the helicop— Oh!" Rose's voice broke through the moment.

They jumped apart and Quinn turned to see her sister standing there, holding a flashlight, and looking more embarrassed then she'd ever seen her look in her life.

"I...I'm sorry. I'll give you guys a moment."

"No, stay," Jeff said. He ran his hands down his jeans. "So, the helicopter is on its way?"

"Yes," Rose said, her eyes looking everywhere but at him and Quinn. "Two helicopters, actually. One to rescue us, and another with law enforcement to apprehend Benny. They've taken off and are about twenty minutes out. The skies are clear enough now for them to drop a rope and pick us up right from the town square."

"That's good," Jeff said. He shifted his weight from one foot to the other awkwardly. "I'm going to go for a quick walk and find Vic. Will you stay here with Addison?"

"Absolutely," Rose said before Quinn could find her voice.

Jeff turned and took off quickly, as if his legs were brand-new and he wasn't quite sure how they worked. It look Quinn a second to realize he'd walked off in the wrong direction and forgotten to take either the flashlight or the walkie-talkie with him.

Her sister gave her a long look and then she plopped down.

"So, what just happened here?" Rose asked.

Quinn sat beside her "Jeff kissed me."

"I saw," Rose said.

"But it was more than that," Quinn said. "I told him about how my business was struggling financially and that I was afraid I'd loose it. He opened up about his past too. We got closer as people." She pressed her elbows into her knees and dropped her head into her hands. "Then he got all weird and awkward."

"Yeah, noticed that too," Rose said. Her sister gently nudged her shoulder.

"What do I do?" Quinn asked, staring at her palms.

"What do you want to do?" Rose replied.

"I don't know," Quinn admitted. She didn't know if Jeff wanted to grow what had started with that fleeting kiss into the kind of real and solid relationship she could build a future around. Even if he did, would he able to? Or would his past always hold him back? She raised her head and looked past her sister to where Addison still lay curled up like a ball sleeping on the floor. But there was one thing she did know for certain. Big Poppa would stop at nothing to exact whatever his evil plan for this little girl. And as long as Quinn was near Jeff and Addison, her future, career, and life would be in jeopardy.

Jeff walked blindly into the night and didn't even realize he'd gone in the opposite direction of the area where Vic was patrolling until he saw the cabin where Addison had been held hostage looming ahead of him. He stopped and turned back. The rain had ceased again, thick trees surrounded him on all sides, and he could hear the sound of the river in the distance as it crashed past the old mill.

His head swam with the knowledge that he'd not only just told the most amazing, unbelievably beautiful and impressive woman he'd ever met all of his darkest secrets, but she'd listened to him, been supportive and admitted some of the stuff she was struggling with too. She'd even held him in her arms and hugged him, instead of pushing him away. Then they'd kissed. In a way that, despite everything else he'd lived through, somehow felt like the first real and genuine kiss he'd ever experienced. And it had been from the one woman he felt he'd never be able to deserve no matter how hard he tried.

Suddenly, he dropped to his knees on the soft, wet ground, as if the full weight of everything burdening his heart had just landed hard on his shoulders. He clasped his hands together behind his head.

"God?" he asked out loud, feeling more like checking to see if someone was within earshot than starting a prayer. "I don't know what I'm doing with my life and I don't know why everything has turned out the way it has. I'm so thankful for Addison and so terrified that I'm not a good enough father. On one level, I know that both Vic and Quinn are right when they tell me I can't blame myself for other people's choices."

He paused and ran his hands over his face. But knowing something in his mind just wasn't enough.

"I don't know why I let Della make me feel unworthy of love," he admitted out loud to God, "or why I beat myself up over my mistakes. But I want to be the kind father who Addison deserves and, one day, I want to be the kind of man who can stand alongside someone like Quinn.

"And I want to stop beating myself up and letting the past run my life. So, I'm asking for help. Help me to let go of the things You don't want me carrying. Please point me in the right direction. Put the people and things in my life that I need to help me do the work I need to do to be a better man. Thanks. Amen."

It wasn't much of a prayer, he thought. Definitely hadn't been anything like the flowery language on the radio station his brother liked listening to. And he wasn't sure he'd remembered to say all the things he'd needed to. But it had been real and honest, and he'd meant every word of it. He sat back on his heels and listened to the river rushing beyond the trees and the faint rustling of the wind in the leaves above him.

As he sat there in silence, a small and simple thought crossed his mind. Everything good he'd accomplished in his life had come slowly and taken time. No matter what his workout might've been on a Monday, being strong enough to serve in the military had still meant getting up the next day, the day after that, and the day after that, and putting himself through his paces all over again. He'd found there was something good, even joyful, in the discipline of the every day. Maybe that's what being a better father and human being was like, and it was something he'd have to rededicate himself to each day for the rest of his life.

And knowing that was enough.

He stood slowly, brushed the dirt off his jeans and started walking back in the direction of the ghost town. He needed to find Quinn, talk to her and apologize for running off like that. While he was at it, he also needed to find his brother and apologize to him too for being so incredibly defensive for the past few months. And then he'd find Addison, cuddle her tightly in his arms and hold her as they waited for rescue.

A flashlight beam flickered through the trees just above his head. Was it Vic? Quinn or Rose? Surely, if rescue had arrived, he would've heard the walkie-talkie. He reached for his walkie-talkie to check in with the others and realized he didn't have it. There was no way to reach out or to get help. So he started walking through the trees toward the light. The trees parted and he saw the old mill, its wheel spinning futilely at the riverside.

"Jeff!" Quinn's voice came faintly through the trees. "Help me! Please. He's going to kill me!"

He looked up at the skeleton of the old mill and saw two shadowy figures on the second floor. A woman was down on her knees. A huge, heavyset man in a shape-less coat and mask loomed tall over her. Big Poppa had Quinn? But how? He'd only left her a few minutes ago, sitting talking with her sister and watching Addison sleep. How had they been invaded? How had Big Poppa lured her away?

Was Addison okay?

"Jeff! Help!" Quinn's scream echoed high-pitched through the night.

"I'm coming!" he shouted. He ran and pushed

through the trees. Something crashed in the distance. He looked up. Big Poppa was gone and now the woman lay sprawled on the ground.

His heart raced. The mill rose ahead of him, two stories tall with missing walls and boards that gaped like a mouth of crooked and missing teeth. He reached the mill, found a ladder and began climbing to the second floor. Rungs spun and cracked under his feet. Silence fell from the floor above him. He prayed for wisdom.

"Jeff! Help!" Quinn's voice was faint.

"I'm coming," he called. "What happened? Are you alone? Are you hurt?"

She didn't answer. He reached the top of the ladder and looked around. The space was empty except for piles of debris in the corner. A small plastic camping lantern on the floor cast the space in an unnatural yellow glow. The mill wheel spun and water crashed beside him, sending spray through the empty space where he guessed a wall had once been, plunging to the river far below. He started across the floor and that's when he saw the body lying directly ahead of him. He steeled a breath and walked toward it. A long black shroud seemed to cover the body. His footsteps reached it, he bent and pulled the fabric back. It was a person-shaped hunting decoy.

What was this?

The blow from behind was so swift and sudden, he pitched forward, landing hard on his hands and knees on the wooden floor beside the dummy. Immediately he sprang back and turned around, his hands raised to strike.

There stood Kelsey with her unnaturally red hair

flying out around her like flames and a small handgun clutched in her hands.

"Kelsey," he said slowly and cautiously, like he was trying to talk down a mountain lion before it struck. "Where's Quinn?"

"Not here," Kelsey snapped.

"But are she and Addison okay?" he asked.

"This has nothing to do with them!" she said. "This is between you and me."

What? Between her and him? What kind of unfinished business could Kelsey possibly think she had with him? Desperation filled her gaze. She pointed the gun right at his chest. And despite the fear pounding inside him, confusion overwhelmed him even more.

Where had she gotten the gun from? Had she had one all this time and just never shown anyone? How had she mimicked Quinn's voice so well? If Kelsey was the woman he'd seen cowering on the ground, how had she rigged the dummy on the floor to look like it was menacing on her?

But above all, he wanted to know…

"Why, Kelsey?" he asked. "Why would you do this? Why did you take my child? Why are you pointing a gun at me? There's never been any bad blood between us. Did I do something to offend you? Or hurt you? If so, I very sincerely apologize."

A thrumming sounded, like a swarm of frustrated mosquitoes trapped in a tin can. Was it the helicopters? Or a drone? Several drones? Watching them? Helping her?

Is that how she'd faked the scene he'd seen?

"Get down!" Kelsey shouted. "Hands up in the air and don't move."

He complied and crouched low, but stayed on the balls of his feet.

"Kelsey, just put the gun down and tell me what's going on," he said. "Let me help you."

"Is it true you killed my dad?" Kelsey demanded.

He started. "What?" he asked. "No, of course not. I've never even met your dad. He died of a heart attack while jogging."

"On a military base!" Kelsey's voice rose. "Benny believed it. Because Dad was so healthy and so strong. There was nothing wrong with him. Then Benny started digging into online groups for people whose loved ones died overseas. And he read there are all sorts of cover-ups and people don't die where they're supposed to and they lie to families. Benny was posting all sorts of questions. Trying to find out the truth."

Unexpected compassion washed over him, imagining a sad and lonely teenager in mourning over the loss of his father having his emotions manipulated and worked up online. He wondered if those were the same chat groups that Paul lost himself in and, for the first time, found himself stopping to wonder just how overwhelmed with anger and sadness Paul must've been to lash out the way he did. Maybe Vic was right and challenging him would've been better than hiding.

"Your brother has a substance abuse problem," Jeff interjected gently. "He needs help and was looking for it in the wrong place. Just because he was reading stuff online doesn't mean the people posting it were telling him the truth."

"Big Poppa found him." Kelsey's voice escalated like she was performing for an unseen audience. "He told us the truth. He told us about you. Big Poppa said he could prove you'd killed people before. Lots of people. He showed us an article about how Addison's mother died—"

"No, Kelsey, I'm sorry," Jeff said, "but he twisted what happened and lied to you—"

"He said there'd been a cover-up and then you'd disappeared." She went on like he hadn't even spoken. "He told us that if we got close to you, we could help him gather the proof he needed to rescue Addison and take her to her real family who loved her. He said he'd take care of her and protect her. And he'd give Benny and me the money we needed to get out of debt, and go to college and get our own place, and start a real life. He said it was perfect because we lived so close to where you were anyway."

"Listen to me," Jeff said, "whoever this Big Poppa person is who contacted you, he lied to you and used you—"

"No, he didn't!" she shouted. Hysteria tinged her voice. "You killed my dad and stole Addison. But Big Poppa told me I can make it right." She yanked the safety off the gun and winced as it tore her skin. Then she raised it between his eyes. "I can fix everything. All I have to do is kill you."

TWELVE

Quinn was walking alone through the woods, following the faint trail in the brush Jeff had left, when she heard the sound of a gunshot shake the night. Terror washed over her like a wave.

Jeff! Desperate prayer filled her head as she turned and ran toward the sound. The trees parted, the old mill came into view and she saw the fight. High above her on the second-story platform, Jeff and Kelsey were wrestling for control of a gun. Their hands stretched up toward the ceiling. The barrel flashed in the light. Then Kelsey yanked back, and Quinn lost sight of the gun. In an instant, Jeff had charged at her again and Quinn realized he was risking his life to try to disarm the young woman without hurting her.

Another bullet fired, followed in quick succession by a second and third.

Had Jeff been shot? Had Kelsey? Then, as she watched, Jeff and Kelsey fell together, through the gap in the wall, past the giant wheel and down into the raging river below.

His name slipped from Quinn's lips in a desperate

cry where it mingled with prayers to God. Quinn turned and scrambled through the trees to the water's edge and the small muddy beach where they'd left the canoes. Rotors spun in the distance. The rescue helicopters were coming. She didn't even turn to turn to look their way. All that mattered now was reaching Jeff. She needed to be by his side. She had to make sure he was okay.

Twin helicopter beams split the darkness behind her, enveloping her in light and illuminating the river. She reached the water's edge and scanned the rapids for any sign of Jeff and Kelsey.

Please, Lord, help me find him. Bring him back to me.

Then she saw him surfacing from the rapids. He was swimming with one strong arm, while holding Kelsey with the other. Exhaustion and worry were etched deeply in the lines of his face and she could tell at a glance he was struggling.

"Jeff!" She shouted his name above the din of the rapids and the roar of the helicopter rotors. "Are you okay?"

"Yes!" he shouted. "But Kelsey's been shot!"

"How?" she called.

By him? By herself? By some third person she hadn't been able to see?

Water swept over him, tossing Jeff and Kelsey under for a long agonizing moment. She could tell he was fighting to keep Kelsey's head above water. He couldn't do it alone. She scanned the remains of her canoe. There was no climbing gear. No rope at all except for the one now tethering her canoe to the shore. Quinn felt for the pocketknife her sister had given her. She whipped it out without hesitation and sliced her canoe free from the rope. Immediately the raging current swept it downstream. She didn't watch it go. Instead, she tied the rope to her belt, doubled-checked it was still tightly tethered to the shore, and waded into the river up to her waist.

"This way!" she shouted. "I've got you!"

He swam toward her and thrust Kelsey's body at her open arms. She caught the young woman's pale and limp form under the elbows. Quinn's knees buckled as the water beat against her legs and, for a moment, almost lost her balance. But Jeff pushed his way to shore, grabbed on to the rope above her and helped pull Kelsey in as she stumbled onto the beach.

Together they lay Kelsey on her back on the ground. Blood and water soaked her clothes. Quinn felt for a pulse at her neck and found it faint. Jeff pushed his hands against the woman's side in what looked like an attempt to cover the gunshot wound and staunch the flow of blood.

"Call Vic," he said. "Tell him to get down here immediately and to alert the paramedics we have a gunshot wound."

She did so, quickly relaying all the details she knew. Then she put the walkie-talkie down and glanced at Jeff. His skin was as ashen as Kelsey's.

"Are you hurt?" she asked.

"No," he said. "Just tired. I didn't shoot her. I didn't even see where the shot came from. I think it was another drone. Someone, somewhere, was watching us." He was so clammy, he looked ready to pass out. "She told me Benny was online a lot after their father died, digging into conspiracy theories. Big Poppa found him there and got them all riled up thinking what they'd been told about their father's death was a lie. Kelsey was hysterical and said Big Poppa told her to kill me. I tried to talk her down and when that didn't work, I tried to wrestle the gun from her. Then a shot came from out of nowhere. I think he was watching the whole thing. I don't know why he shot her, though. Maybe he was trying to shoot me."

Suddenly they were surrounded by Canadian Rangers' search and rescue.

Quinn and Jeff stepped back as paramedics took over care of Kelsey. Jeff looked down at his shirt, stained pink from his attempts to stop the bleeding. "I've got to get changed before Addison sees me and gets frightened," he said. "Find your sister and let's get out of here. Just remember, Big Poppa could be watching us from anywhere. Never assume you're alone."

Her arms ached to hug him, but he disappeared into the crowd. She was still scanning for him when a ranger in a red cardigan came up beside her and draped a rescue blanket across her shoulders.

"Don't worry, ma'am," he said with a reassuring smile. "It's all over."

She almost laughed. Addison had thankfully been rescued. And even if Quinn's campers didn't sue her into the ground over what had happened, her company and dream of being a wilderness guide were as good as dead.

But something told her that as long as Big Poppa was out there, Jeff's ordeal would never truly be over.

Lord, please bring this nightmare to an end.

Rose found Quinn before Quinn found her.

Less than twenty minutes later, another ranger was leading them through the woods to the evacuation point where a third ranger helped them into a helicopter. To her surprise, she was the last one to arrive and found Jeff, Addison, Vic and the puppy all there waiting for them. With the exception of the dog, they were all wearing headphones to block out the noise with microphones to allow them to talk.

"Daddy and I flew!" Addison pronounced sleepily under heavily lidded eyes. Her voice was all but swallowed up by the sound of the rotors. "We went whoosh like a super'ero." She turned to her father who was sitting in the seat beside hers, the dog on his lap. "Right, Daddy? You fly!"

"I'm not a superhero, sweetie…" Jeff started.

"But your daddy is a hero," Vic said. "He's a Canadian Ranger like the brave men and women helping us."

Jeff nodded and closed his eyes. But Vic's words hit Quinn like a dart. While she hadn't exactly forgotten that Jeff was a ranger, the full implication of that had slipped her mind. At some point in the not too distant future, Jeff would be deploying for a few weeks of service at a time, not to mention being on call in case of major disasters. If it had been another person's daughter who'd been kidnapped on this trip, Jeff would've probably been called in to help with the rescue.

Quinn's gaze fell on the precious little girl. What would happen to Addison when Jeff was called up to serve his country? Who would keep her safe?

The helicopters ride was choppy, and it wasn't too long before Addison declared she did not like the "loud plane" and wanted to land immediately. Quinn knew how Addison felt. Her entire body ached to sleep. Even greater than that was her desire to just sit somewhere quiet with Jeff, give him a hug and talk. She didn't know what she wanted to say or how to begin to explain just how much he meant to her, let alone admit her fear that he might never be ready to be the kind of man she could see in her future. All she knew was that she'd never been able to forget him and the idea of saying goodbye again and going their separate ways made something ache deep inside her chest.

But she couldn't discuss that with him now, in a noisy helicopter, in front of their siblings and his daughter, even if she had been able to find the words to say. So instead, she just glanced out the window and stared at the dark treetops billowing like waves below her and prayed.

They started to descend far sooner than she'd expected them to and looked out to see a myriad of golden lights spread out beneath them, like a small village of cottages and lodges, hidden deep in the forest. Rose had told her that someone connected to Leia's fiancé had offered her campers a place to stay only a few hours away from the cabin. She'd never imagined it would be a huge resort with its own helicopter pad rimmed in spotlights. The landing was smooth.

A ranger in the front seat leaped out, came around and opened the back door for them. Quinn saw a striking woman with long dark hair clad in a stunning bright yellow jacket striding toward them, flanked by two men in suits and several uniformed members of the Royal Canadian Mounted Police. Quinn let the ranger help her out and escort her under the slowing rotors. She met the woman in yellow at the edge of the helicopter pad.

"You must be Quinn," the woman said as she reached for Quinn's hand. "I'm Sunny Shields. Welcome to the site of Shields' new Muskoka resort. I'm afraid we're still under construction, but thankfully our main lodge is complete and able to accommodate your campers."

"Thank you," Quinn said. She suspected that sheer crushing exhaustion was the only thing keeping her from completely reeling at the fact she was now shaking hands with one of the wealthiest and most powerful women in the country. "I can't begin to thank you for stepping in like that to take care and help rescue my campers."

"Not a problem." Sunny smiled. "We had plenty of extra space."

Quinn was amused to see that Rose's mouth gaped as she came to join them. Apparently, Rose hadn't known who their benefactor was either, and she imagined that when they reunited their older sister, Leia was going to get quite the grilling on who exactly in her fiancé's contacts circle knew a friend of Sunny Shields'.

But Quinn's smile began to fade when the uniformed officers pulled Jeff and Vic aside, only to disappear entirely when she saw Jeff frown. Whatever the police were telling Jeff, it was bad news. And it took all the self-control Quinn had to turn her back and let Sunny lead her across the lawn. They walked along a beautiful stone walkway with inset lights up to a huge wooden lodge, like a far fancier and grander version of Jeff's log cabin in the woods.

Another man opened the door for them and Quinn

wondered just how many people Sunny had working this late at night. She couldn't remember the last time she'd seen a clock or a watch, but judging by fatigue alone, Quinn guessed it had to be approaching two in the morning.

They walked into the lodge, past an empty, glossy concierge counter that looked somehow hewn from a single piece of wood. She expected to be led into some kind of office, but instead Sunny pushed through a set of beautiful double doors into a dazzling ballroom encircled by floor-to-ceiling windows on three sides.

Quinn heard the applause before her eyes even registered who was doing the clapping. There was every single one of her campers, alive, well and leaping to their feet, giving her a standing ovation. And until that moment she had no idea just how much something inside her had needed to see their faces. Tears filled her eyes. Tables were dotted around the room with half-filled platters of sandwiches, cheeses, pastries, pitchers of water and pots of coffee, making her wonder just how long had they all been sitting there waiting for her.

"You made it!" Marcel broke through the group, bounded across the room and threw his arms around Quinn. He hugged her so hard, he practically lifted her off the floor. "Did you use my maps?"

"I did!" She laughed. "But I'm sorry, I lost them."

"That's okay," he said and stepped back. His smile beamed. "I've got backups on my computer."

At that, the group broke up as campers came by to hug them, clasp their hands or exchange a fist bump before filtering back to their tables, laptops and cell phones.

"Aren't you a sight for sore eyes," Kirk said. "None of us were about to go sleep until we'd make sure you were okay." The old man chuckled and slapped her on the shoulder. For a guy in his sixties, he was surprisingly strong. "Where's the little whippersnapper?"

"Addison? Yeah." She'd forgotten how Kirk had said Addison reminded him of his granddaughter. "She's with her dad and uncle."

Who were now talking to law enforcement about something that Jeff seemed worried about. She hoped everything was okay.

"That's good." Kirk nodded. "A little girl like that belongs with her family."

"She does," Quinn said. But where did Jeff think she fit into that picture? And where did she want to fit?

Quinn and her sister moved through the room, making small talk and chatting about what they'd all been through in the past day, like butterflies dancing over the surface of a difficult conversation without ever landing. Somebody pushed food into her hands. She took a few bites without even tasting it. Rose called Leia and Sally again with another update.

Quinn felt a chill of cold night air and turned.

A door was open in the wall of glass windows that looked out over the lawn. Jeff stood there alone in the doorway. His serious eyes alighted on her. Without a word, she turned and walked over to him.

"Hey," he said and her heart froze to see the look of dread on his face. "Do you have a minute? We need to talk."

She nodded and followed him outside. The door

swung shut behind them. They walked slowly away from the lodge and along the grass.

"Police finally have Paul in custody," Jeff said. "And I was wrong this whole time. He's been ruled out completely. So has Pastor Drew."

A small lake rippled ahead of them. Golden lights danced on the calm surface of the pitch-black water.

"We've exhausted every lead and I'm at a complete loss," he said. "Law enforcement has no idea who has been hunting my daughter and the nightmare is nowhere near over."

As they walked down to the waterfront together, somehow Jeff's hand kept finding hers. He wasn't intentionally reaching for her hand, let alone trying to take it. But somehow their fingers kept brushing and their arms kept bumping into each other, as if their hands wanted to link but neither of them was willing to make the first move.

"How do you know it's not Paul?" she asked. "You were so convinced it was him, and they couldn't find him for so long."

"Turns out he's on a cruise ship off the coast of Hawaii on his honeymoon," Jeff said. He blew out a long breath. "He's in love. He and his fiancée eloped with their parents in tow, had a beachfront wedding, and are now on a cruise. Detectives actually got through to him and interviewed not only Paul, but his wife, the ship's captain, his parents and in-laws. He's been off the grid for days and there's literally no way he could've done this, even if he'd wanted to."

The irony of which wasn't lost on him for a moment.

In his mind, Paul had remained locked in his worst moment. To Jeff, the other man was almost rabid with anger and pain. When in reality, Paul had moved on, leaving Jeff afraid of an enemy who was no longer lurking in the shadows waiting to strike. But then, if he was wrong about Paul, who was Big Poppa?

An intricate wrought-iron bench stood a few feet by the waterfront. She walked over to it and sat. He paused at the side of the bench, debated sitting beside her, and then decided to continue to stand.

"Where do we go from here?" she asked.

"Well, Vic and I are leaving right away to take Addison back to the cabin," he said. "The resort has arranged a rental car for us. Vic is getting Addison and Butterscotch into the car now. They're just waiting for me to join them, and then we're going to go. Should only take us about three hours. I think it's important that life returns to normal for Addison as soon as possible, and that after everything she went through today, she wake up in her own bed tomorrow. My brother and I need to sit down together and figure out what we're going to do about the whole situation."

"So, where does that leave us?" she asked.

Jeff stepped back and stared into the face of the most beautiful, amazing and incredible woman he'd ever laid eyes on. Worry filled her eyes but a brave smile crossed her face. And his heart sank with the knowledge of the words he was going to have to say.

He swallowed hard and forced the words he didn't want to say past his lips.

Please understand, I don't want to do this. But I have to. It's the only way.

"There is no us in this anymore," he said.

Jeff watched as feelings flickered through her eyes like a kaleidoscope of emotions. But when she spoke, her words were remarkably direct.

Her arms crossed. "What exactly are you saying?"

She wasn't about to make this easy on him, was she? Didn't she understand that pushing her away was the only way to keep them all safe?

"I talked to Vic about this whole situation and the threats against our lives," he said. "My whole focus has to be on what's best for Addison and I can't afford any distractions. So, I don't think we should be in each other's lives after tonight. We're better, and safer, apart."

She blew out a long breath like she was weighing her words before speaking them. Then her head shook.

"I don't believe you," she said and stood. "Because if this was really about what's good for me, you'd be asking my opinion instead of making decisions for me. Plus, you know we're stronger together, and pushing me out of your life is not going to help or to make you or Addison safer. So, if you're going to kick me out of your life, then the least you owe me is an honest answer. I deserve that."

He'd braced himself for sadness. He'd expected her to be disappointed and confused—maybe she'd even cry a bit—and he'd do his best to comfort her. He hadn't been expecting whatever this was. It was almost anger.

"This." He waved his hand in the air between them as if tracing invisible lines. "Whatever this thing, this connection, is between us, it's a liability. Big Poppa used Kelsey and Benny to get to me and Addison, probably just because they lived near me geographically.

We still have no idea who Big Poppa is. I've still got a target on my back and being around me puts your life at jeopardy—"

Fire flashed in her eyes. "And you don't think I'm willing to risk that?"

"Maybe you are—" his voice rose "—but I'm not! As long as you are in my life, we're both in danger. For some reason, he used you and your wilderness adventure company as a vehicle to snatch my daughter away from me, and I still don't know why. He used what I can only assume was a doctored audio of your voice to lure me to the mill to make me think that Kelsey was you so that she could kill me. Who's to stop him from trying to use you to hurt me again? Or from using me to hurt you?" Then his voice dropped so low it was almost a whisper. "I care about you so much, Quinn. You make me vulnerable. Can't you see that?"

She pressed her lips together and nodded slowly. But more like she was parsing her thoughts than agreeing with him.

"So, you're willing to let your fear or some faceless criminal dictate what you're going to do with your life," she said. "I'm sorry for you. Because if that's really what you think—and you're not saying all this for some other reason I don't understand—then you're not the man I thought you were and I don't want this in my life either."

She turned to go, without even saying goodbye, her verbal sucker punch leaving him winded.

"Wait!" Jeff took two paces after her. She turned back and he reached into his pocket and pulled out a small piece of paper. "I want you to have this."

She unfolded it slowly.

"It's a check," she said.

"For twenty thousand dollars," he said. "Made out to your company."

"Yeah, I can see that." She stared at the paper. Her voice was flat.

"You told me you'd been struggling financially and might lose your wilderness tour business," he said, "and I felt at least partially responsible for that—"

At that, her gaze snapped up to his face. "Because we were being honest and open with each other about our lives. Not because I wanted your pity!"

"It's an investment," he said. "In you, because I believe in you. It's from a joint investment account I have with Vic and, thankfully, he had some checks in his wallet. The routing and account information is right there. Just deposit back what you can, whenever you can, however long it takes."

"No." She ripped the check in two. "I'm not taking your money. And if you knew me as well as I thought you did, you'd know I want to rise or fall on my own merits. If my company dies, I want to be the one to find a way to fix it. Not just let somebody bail me out."

She kept tearing the check into smaller and smaller pieces.

"I'm not about to let you take the coward's way out either," she said. "Or make yourself feel better about hurting me because you'll know your money is out there helping me live my dreams. If you want to be in my life, Jeff, be in my life. Caring about someone is always a risk, even when there isn't some killer on the loose. My father risked his life to marry my mother and raise us girls. He put everything on the line to love my sisters and me. Your brothers and sisters in uniform overseas and in the Canadian Rangers put their lives on the line for each other, their country and strangers every day. So, step up, risk hurting me, and risk being hurt. Or don't. Your choice. But I can't keep letting myself be emotionally drawn deeper and deeper toward someone who's not willing to do the same for me."

"Quinn." His hands reached out into the space between them. His heart ached to make her understand. She had to know how he felt about her. She had to know he hated this every bit as much as she did. But it was the only way.

Then, before he could say another word, she turned and strode across the lawn toward the lodge, leaving nothing but the remains of his check scattered like confetti at his feet, and either the real or imagined very faint sound of something metallic whirring in the darkness.

THIRTEEN

Hot tears stung her eyes. She wiped them away as she strode back to the lodge, before any of her campers could see them. Behind her, she could hear Jeff calling her name. She didn't look back. So much for worrying that he'd break her heart. He'd turned and run before he'd even let them get that close.

She reached the door and paused, closed her eyes tightly, took a deep breath in and let it out slowly. Why had Jeff acted that way? Had he been watching his words in case Big Poppa was listening? Maybe he had. Maybe Jeff had done what he'd done out of a genuine desire to help her and save her? But even if he had, even if his heart had been completely in the right place, she needed the kind of man who'd stand beside her no matter what hit them, not the kind who thought he was helping her by pushing her away.

Lord, I'm afraid my heart might never stop feeling for him the way I do about Jeff. I've asked You so many times to take these feelings away from me. But even if You don't, and I'm going to have to learn to walk

*through this pain, help me to be wise. And please keep
Jeff and Addison safe.*

She opened her eyes then opened the door and
walked into the ballroom. An awkward silence greeted
her. Gone was the relaxed, relieved and cheerful at-
mosphere that had filled the room when she'd left it.
Now people had their eyes locked on their computers
or huddled in twos and threes in front of screens ex-
changing hushed whispers as if they were watching
some tragedy unfold.

Rose crossed the floor toward her and pulled her
aside. Her sister's face was pale.

"What's going on?" Quinn asked.

"Somebody posted a heavily edited video of Jeff and
Kelsey's confrontation online," Rose said, keeping her
voice low. "It makes it look like Kelsey told Jeff that she
knew he was involved in the deaths of his unit overseas
and then he murdered her."

"What?" Quinn gasped. Her mind reeled. "Did
Kelsey die?"

"Not that I know of," Rose said. "The paramedics
who airlifted her said that she was in stable condition
and expected to survive her injuries. But this has nothing to do with the truth. This is about making Jeff out
to be a killer."

Quinn turned, ran to the door, pushed it open and
rushed out into the night. Jeff was gone. She turned
back and Rose was waiting for her in the doorway.

"I don't think Big Poppa is trying to kill him," Quinn
said. "He's trying to destroy Jeff's life and take everything from him. He could've had Jeff murdered and
taken Addison, but instead left him alive to experi-

ence the pain of what he'd lost. I don't even think he expected Kelsey to kill Jeff. He was setting him up to look like a killer."

She was pretty sure that Jeff didn't know anything about the video and, depending when he and Vic eventually went online, it might be hours and hours before they found out about it. Hours that the video would sit online unchallenged and Big Poppa could use it to whip up more people to help him in his quest to dismantle Jeff's life.

Benny's angry words back in the cabin echoed in her mind.

Thirty thousand dollars for the little girl alive... Ten thousand if she's dead.

This had never been about giving Addison a new home. Yes, Big Poppa had wanted to have her and might've convinced himself he'd be a better dad than Jeff would ever be. But even more than that, he'd wanted to hurt Jeff. No, more than that he wanted to utterly destroy him. In any way he could. And now that he'd lost his grip on the little girl, just how far would he go? She and Jeff might not have a future together, but that wasn't going to stop her from doing whatever she could to protect his daughter and save his life, especially as he might have no idea this video even existed.

"Quinn, are you okay?" Kirk called from the doorway. "Is there anything I can do to help?"

"Yes," she said. "Please run, find the parking lot and see if you can still catch Jeff. Apparently he's borrowed a vehicle and hopefully he hasn't left yet. If you see him, please tell him I need to see him right away."

"Will do." Kirk turned and jogged off into the night.

She turned to Rose. "That's a good start, but we're going to need more help than that. Did you happen to bring your laptop with you on this trip?"

Rose shook her head. "Sorry, just my phone."

"I just have my tablet," Quinn said. And that was somewhere in her luggage, which she hadn't even been reunited with yet, as it was probably in her room, wherever that was. "Thankfully, I know exactly who I can ask for that."

She rushed back into the ballroom and found Marcel sitting at a corner table, his eyes locked on the screen. He closed the screen when he saw her coming, but not before she caught a glimpse of the video of Jeff and Kelsey he was watching.

"I'm sorry," Marcel said and blushed. "I'll turn it off."

"No, don't," Quinn said. "I need you to keep it playing and come with me. We need your help."

He nodded and followed her out of the ballroom and back into the hallway, along with Rose. The lobby was empty now. Vacant offices lined one of the walls, with large frosted windows looking out into the main area. She led them into one of them and closed the door.

The desk was so new it still had cardboard and bubble wrap protecting the legs. Wooden chairs were stacked in one corner. She grabbed the top one, placed it in front of the desk and waved Marcel into it.

"I need you to save everything you can get your hands on about that video, who posted it and how it was created, before someone deletes it," she said. "Then I need you to open a secure video chat channel." She glanced at her sister. "Can you send Leia a message

and ask her if there's a way we can get in touch with
her fiancé?"

Rose typed a message and a whoosh sounded followed by a ping.

"He's still hanging out at the farmhouse," she said.
She gave Marcel the number and he set up the video
call. It rang.

"Thank you for trusting me," Marcel whispered.

"No problem." Quinn smiled and silently prayed her
instincts about him were right.

A second later, a window opened on the screen and
she looked to see her dark-haired sister Leia and her fiancé, Jay, sitting at the dining room table in the Dukes
family farmhouse, giant mugs of what looked like coffee in front of them.

"So, no one is sleeping tonight," Quinn said after
she and Rose had said their hellos and given a quick
update on what they'd missed since they'd last spoken.

"Oh, the whole gang is here," Leia said. She picked
up the laptop and turned it around so that they could
see about a dozen people scattered around the living
room. Then she turned it back to her face. "Nobody
was about to go home until we knew you'd made it to
the hotel safe."

"And by then we were all too tired to drive," quipped
a man with scraggly blond hair. "Hence the coffee."

"Do you know how to reach that tech contact who
works on cases with police and knows how to find
pretty much anything online?" Quinn asked.

"Yo!" The coffee man raised his hand. "I'm Seth.
What do you need?"

She let out a long breath and thanked God.

Seth pulled a laptop from somewhere off screen and came to join Leia at the table.

"My friend Marcel is going to send through everything he can pull on a video link," Quinn said. "We need to know everything we can about who filmed, edited and posted it, and make sure it's relayed to police."

He nodded.

Leia's fiancé gestured to a short woman with long blond hair and a tight, round pregnancy belly that looked at least eight months on. "Jess here is a detective with the Ontario Provincial Police specializing in special victim cases. She's already been coordinating with the lead detective on the case."

Joy filled Quinn's heart, as unexpectedly the memory of being kidnapped by Benny filled her mind. She'd felt so completely and utterly alone when she'd been tied to the tree. She'd had no idea she had this team of people behind her.

Conversations had already started to flow between the various people on both sides of the screen. The room filled with the sound of keyboards clacking. Quinn grabbed a hotel notebook and pen from the desk and did her best to draw the drone she'd seen from memory.

"Also, can someone track this?" she asked.

"Will do," Leia said.

"Can you get someone to email through a list of all of the people on your camping trip?" Jess the detective called from the corner of the screen. "Focus on anyone who was out of Rose's sight at any point today and could've made a secret call if they had a satellite phone. My detective contact said the investigators were having trouble tracking everyone for cross referencing."

"Will do," Quinn said. A knock sounded on the door. She looked up to see Kirk's flushed face looking in the partially frosted window. Had he found Jeff? She glanced at Rose. "I've got to talk to Kirk. Can you take over point on that?"

Rose smiled. "Absolutely."

Quinn waved at the people on the screen and then stepped out into the hallway. Kirk was alone. "I'm guessing you didn't find Jeff?"

"Oh, no, I sure did," Kirk said. "Sorry it took so long but I searched the wrong parking lot at first. His baby girl is asleep. He doesn't want to wake her up and he doesn't want to leave her. So I told him I'd go get you."

"Thanks," she said.

She followed him down the hallway in the opposite direction of the lobby.

"I'm so glad that you and Jeff are back working together again," Kirk said.

He pushed out a fire door into the night. The parking lot loomed large and empty in front of them. He led her past the smattering of vehicles by the front entrance that she assumed belonged to Sunny's staff, and toward a large car, its lights on, parked on the far side of the lot.

"I still remember going on that trip you guys ran together two years ago," Kirk added. "You and Jeff had such great chemistry back then. You could tell you two were a great fit. That's why I looked you up when you both left, and you started your own company"

Yeah, she remembered that Kirk had asked her back then if she knew where Jeff was or if they were planning any trips together. In fact, he was the only camper she'd met at their previous tour company who'd ever asked where Jeff was or how he was doing.

Then she realized that, although Kirk liked to talk up being a grandfather, she'd never once seen a picture of the kid.

She glanced back. The lodge was much farther away than the vehicle ahead now, but something told her that Jeff might not be in that car and there was a whole lot of empty space stretched out around her. She reached into her pocket and felt for her knife.

"You know, I've never met your granddaughter," she said. "Kate was it?"

"Catherine," Kirk said and frowned. "Named after my mother. Not like—"

"Those awful modern names they come up with nowadays." Quinn finished the thought for him. He stopped walking and turned to look at her. "Yes, you've said that before."

Jeff had told her that Della had an abusive, controlling father who'd been in the military, and that Addison's mother had gone so far as to get a restraining order against him to keep him out of her and Della's life. Had they thought he was gone from their lives?

Or that he might come for his granddaughter.

"So, I'm guessing you don't like the name Addison?" she asked.

His ugly scowl told her everything she needed to know. She tightened her grip on her knife. If only she hadn't come out here with him. Now, there was nowhere to run. There was nowhere to hide. No way to call for help. The only thing she could do was stand her ground and fight.

"What about Della?" she asked.

"Her name is Adelle!" Kirk's voice rose. "I called her Adelle! She had no right to change it to Della!"

"So, you're Addison's poppa," Quinn said. "Addison is the Catherine you keep talking about. Did you call her that because you didn't like the name your daughter had given her? To hide the truth? Or both?"

He didn't answer. They'd been so busy thinking about "poppa" as a father they hadn't even stopped to think Big Poppa could be Addison's grandfather. "You think Jeff took her from you?"

"My stupid former wife *gave* her to him!" Kirk snarled. "After he'd killed my baby girl, before I could make Della see that it was her mother who'd loaded her head with lies. Her mother poisoned her against me. I don't even find out I'm a grandfather until my daughter is already dead. And then, my ex-wife just hands my granddaughter off to him."

"Jeff is Addison's father—"

"She's my granddaughter!" he snapped. Darkness filled his eyes as he narrowed his gaze. "My blood!"

She yanked the knife from her pocket. But it was too late. Kirk raised a Taser and fired. The prongs dug like pincers into her skin. Electricity shot like fire through her veins. Desperate prayers filled her mind. She crumbled to the ground, unable to do more than whimper as the old man clamped a chloroform-soaked rag over her mouth and nose.

Unconsciousness took over Quinn's body, blocking out the pain.

She felt her body being carried, her hands being tied, and the rumble of a car shaking through her body.

She heard her own screams echoing around her from the darkness and realized he'd locked her in a trunk. She slept fitfully, waking for brief moments as she drifted from one nightmare to another. Time passed. He couldn't just take her without being known. Rose would realize she was gone and call the police. They'd know the last person she'd been seen with was Kirk, and find him missing, along with the vehicle, whether he'd borrowed or stolen it.

One way or another, she'd eventually be found and the police would know exactly who'd taken her. He couldn't possibly expect to get away with it. Then a fresh fear filled her mind. What if he wasn't trying to get away with it? What if wherever he was taking her, he wasn't planning on ever coming back?

Finally, the vehicle stopped. The trunk opened. Pale morning sunlight trickled through thick pine trees. And before she could brace herself to run, she saw Kirk standing there, pointing a gun at her face.

"Let's go," he said. "It's time to end this. Don't do anything stupid or I will hurt you."

She nodded to show that she'd heard him but knew in her heart that she'd never comply. The first opportunity she got, she would fight, she would run, and she'd battle to her final breath to escape from him alive. She climbed out and stumbled to the ground. He grabbed her arm and hauled her to her feet. Then he moved his left hand to her shoulder as he used the right to dig the gun into her ribs.

"Walk," he ordered. He steered her down a path and suddenly she realized where he had taken her. They were back where they'd started the morning before, standing outside Jeff's cabin. She wondered if the reason he hadn't gagged her was that he wanted Jeff to hear her beg for her life, and promised herself she wouldn't give him the satisfaction.

He propelled her forward and she stumbled up the front steps. Kirk let go of her shoulder and knocked hard on the door. It swung open under his touch.

There stood Jeff, right in the middle of his living room, as if he'd been caught unawares while crossing the room.

Addison was curled up asleep behind him on the couch, buried so deeply under the blankets all Quinn could see was her golden curls peeking out the top. The sound of her gentle breathing rose and fell from under the blankets. She couldn't see Butterscotch anywhere. Or Vic.

Jeff's blue eyes locked on hers as Kirk pushed her through the door and into the cabin, never leaving her face for a moment. Their depths filled with fierce and protective compassion that took her breath away. His arms crossed in front of his chest as he stood between Kirk and little Addison, and Quinn knew in that moment she'd never seen anyone look stronger.

"Hey, Quinn," he said softly, as if the man holding a gun against her didn't matter at all. "I was wrong, and you were right. We should've done this together. And no, not because Kirk's got a gun shoved into your side. But because every moment since I said goodbye I've missed you and known I would've done so much better if we'd been together. I'm sorry I ever made you doubt I'd be willing to take a bullet for you."

She knew in that moment his heart was open and that

he was telling her the truth. Chills coursed down her spine like a waterfall, but when she opened her mouth, no words came out.

Then Jeff cut his eyes to the man holding her at gunpoint.

"Feel free to skip whatever big revenge speech you've been practicing in your head," Jeff said. His lip curled in distain. "I know who you are, Big Poppa. And now, so do the police. Thanks to everything Quinn provided her family and friends, they figured out you'd bought the drones, and found your search history as well as the fake online accounts you used to bribe and blackmail people into helping you. Detectives contacted your ex-wife and confirmed your true identity as Addison's grandfather. They all worked very hard and were incredibly busy in the past three hours it took you to drive here. You wouldn't believe how many calls I've been on. Quinn's detective friends are the ones who figured out who you were, thanks to everyone she'd given them, and Addison's grandmother confirmed it. I let police know moment you pulled up and they're on their way here to arrest you right now for kidnapping, murder and attempted murder. You are not leaving here a free man."

Kirk snarled. "You know as well as I do it'll take the police over an hour to get here, and by then I'll be done." He shoved Quinn by the shoulder. "Go stand over there by the end of the couch, near the kid's feet."

She watched as Jeff slowly nodded as if telling her to do what Kirk said. She walked to the end of the couch. Kirk swung his gun back and forth between the top of Addison's curly head and Quinn's face.

"How long did it take you to set this all up?" Jeff asked. "Two years? Ever since the first camp you met me on even before I had custody of Addison? Is that how long you've been planning your revenge? Did you ever stop to think about the people whose lives you were ruining on your quest? Innocent people who did nothing to you like Bruno, Kelsey, Benny and Quinn."

"You took everything from me, Jeff," Kirk said, and she wondered just how many hours he'd spent rehearsing this moment in his mind only for Jeff to refuse to be cowed into listening to him now. "First, my daughter, then my granddaughter—"

"I took nothing from you." Jeff's voice climbed. "You lost it all on your own by hurting those who love you. Your ex-wife, Addison's grandmother, gave me a message to give you. God loves you. Even though I'd just woken her up in the middle of the night with the news about her granddaughter having been kidnapped and rescued, and that we needed her help to confirm your identity, she wants you to know that God hasn't given up on you. All you've got to do is put the gun down and be willing to change."

"Shut up!" Kirk snapped. "That woman poisoned my daughter, gave you my granddaughter, and destroyed my life. I don't care what she says right now."

"She said you'd say that too," Jeff said. "But I promised her I'd try."

"I'm done talking." The barrel of Kirk's gun ticked back and forth from Addison to Quinn again. "It's time for you to choose which one I kill. Your daughter or Quinn. Who lives and who dies."

"Jeff…" Quinn started. But as Jeff glanced at her

face, his name froze on her tongue. She knew that he already knew what she was going to say. Jeff knew she would take a bullet for her daughter and it meant more to him than he'd ever be able to express.

"No, Kirk," Jeff said. "Or Big Poppa, or whoever you want to pretend to be. I don't care how long you've spent dreaming up your sick and twisted revenge. I'm not playing your game."

"Then let's just jump to the end."

Kirk's mouth twisted into an ugly smile. He turned and fired at the sleeping child.

The bullets shredded the pink and pastel blankets and pillows, destroying the giant golden-haired doll and audio recorder Jeff had set up as a decoy. Big Poppa wasn't the only one capable of using props and technology to trick people into seeing what he wanted them to see. The sound of Quinn's horrified cry as Kirk emptied his clip at what she thought was Addison stung like a dagger in Jeff's heart, but he had to wait to hold her. Now he had a killer to stop.

Kirk swore suddenly as he was hit by the realization that he'd been fooled. But it was too late. Jeff tackled him to the ground. He pulled his head back as Kirk fought hard, landing blow after blow at Jeff's shoulders and chest. He was surprisingly strong, and incredibly fit, but no match for Jeff. He wrestled Kirk over onto his stomach. The older man's right hand dug deep into his pocket, like he was reaching for something. But Jeff didn't give him time to pull it out. He pinned him there and yanked his hands hard behind his back. Kirk struggled and swore.

"Quinn!" Jeff shouted. "Help! There's a pack of zip ties hidden under the pillow on the chair."

Then she realized she still her hands tied. Quinn kicked the chair over, caught the ties with her foot before they could fly across the floor and place-kicked them over to Jeff.

"Impressive kick," he said.

"Thanks," Quinn managed to huff, and he realized she was still hyperventilating from the trauma.

He handcuffed Kirk at the wrists and then bound his ankles as the man tried to kick at him.

Jeff leaped to his feet, ran to Quinn and pulled her into his arms.

"It's okay," Jeff said. He reached behind her without ending the embrace and used his pocketknife to free her wrists from their bonds. Then he took her hand and led her out of the cabin and away from the criminal swearing and thrashing on his living room floor. The door shut behind them.

"I'm so sorry for scaring you like that," he said. He wrapped his arms around her again and felt her lay her head against his chest. "Addison was never in any danger. She and the puppy are safe with Vic. Law enforcement has the area surrounded from a safe distance. Rescue is just seconds away. But I meant every word I said earlier. I knew Big Poppa was never going to stop and the only way out was to lure him into a sting. I never should've tried to do it without you. I missed you every second and I promise I will never push you out again." His hands rose to her face. "Forgive me?"

A smile crossed her lips and illuminated her eyes.

"I do," she said. "But no more crime fighting without me."

He chuckled. "I won't, I promise." He pulled back just enough to reach into his pocket and grab a walkie-talkie. He held it to his ear. "We got him. No injuries. All went pretty smoothly. Despite the fact he shot up the decoy he thought was my daughter."

Jeff's teeth clenched in rage at the memory. But he took a deep breath and let thankfulness flow through him. Big Poppa had been stopped. It was finally over.

Something whizzed through the air past him and struck his cabin. The window shattered. The smell of smoke filled the air. Before he could even react, a second explosion hit the tree beside them, making it burst into flames.

"Drones!" Quinn shouted and pointed to the small metallic crafts hovering in the air.

Big Poppa must've activated them when he reached into his pocket, deciding he'd rather die alongside Jeff then let him live his life in peace. Well, Jeff wasn't about to let that happen. He grabbed both of Quinn's hands in his and held them tightly.

"I need you," he said urgently. "I don't think I can do this on my own."

"I'm with you to the end," she said, and he knew with absolute certainty it was true.

He brushed a kiss on her lips, dropped her hands and they back ran into the cabin. Smoke billowed toward him, mingled with the ugly sound of Kirk laughing. Fire licked around the side of the room and rose to the ceiling. In moments, everything he owned would be engulfed in flames. Jeff covered his face with his shirt, grabbed Kirk by one arm, Quinn grabbed him by the other, and they dragged him out into the forest and away from the cabin. Jeff yanked the criminal to his feet and slung him over his shoulder in a fireman's carry.

"I'm not going to be the one who kills him," Jeff told Quinn. "I've never been a killer and he's not going to make me one. I've got a cistern. It's got reinforced walls, it's shallow enough that he won't drown and wide enough he'll survive until rescue arrives."

Quinn followed him as he ran and dropped the man inside, ignoring the torrent of swearwords Kirk spewed.

"We won't fit in there with him," he said, "even if I wanted to."

"What about the river?" Quinn asked.

A thunderous crash sounded as a tree fell through the cabin roof. Jeff felt Quinn's hand tighten in his. Without looking back, he and Quinn turned and ran through the forest, away from the criminal who'd tried to destroy his life, and the remains of the home Jeff had built to hide away from the outside world. They raced toward the river. The smell of the fire engulfed them. The heat of the flames beat against his back. Memories filled his mind again of the deaths he'd seen overseas and the lives that had been lost, threatening to overwhelm his vision.

"Don't let go of my hand!" he shouted.

"I won't," Quinn called and he felt her grip tighten. "I promise."

The cliff side loomed ahead of them and they leaped. Their bodies fell through the air in unison and hit the water. He went under, felt her hand pull from his, and forced his way to the surface.

"Jeff!" she shouted. He looked to see her climbing onto a small island, no more than a couple of feet wide, that jutted from the water ahead. "This way!"

He swam for it. Jeff grabbed hold of the rough scrub growing from the granite with one hand, she grabbed his other hand and helped pull him up.

There they stood, toe to toe and nose to nose, safe on a tiny piece of ground not much larger than a dining room chair. Water roared past them, kicking up spray at their feet. Smoke rose above them and flames licked the top of the trees.

He startled a ring sounded from his pocket. He pulled out his phone. "Hello?"

"Jeff!" his brother's voice boomed down the phone. "Rescuers just pulled Kirk from our cistern and arrested him. Where are you?"

"Standing on a rock in the river."

"With Quinn?"

"Absolutely," Jeff said and felt himself smile. "I've got her right here with me."

"Hold tight," Vic said. "Rescue is on its way."

He heard Quinn whisper a prayer of thanksgiving as he ended the call and he echoed it in his own heart. Then her hands slid around his neck and he wrapped his around her waist and held her to him.

"I'm sorry about your cabin," she said.

"Cabins can be replaced," he said. He looked down at her. "But this thing between us? You?" His voice choked in his throat. "You're irreplaceable. You're the most incredible person I've ever known. I need you in my life. Addison needs you. I'm in love with you, Quinn, and

I know if I don't fight for us, I'm going to regret it for the rest of my life."

"I love you too," she whispered. "Maybe I always have, and I don't ever want to lose you."

"Then I'm going to have to do what it takes to make sure you never do," he said.

She stood on tiptoes and kissed his lips as he heard the sound of rescue helicopters circling above.

FOURTEEN

The fire had burned for three days, taking out a huge swath of the Ontario forest, and hundreds of Canadian Rangers had been mobilized along with firefighters to evacuate the town, care for those displaced and tackle the blaze. These were his people, Jeff thought as he sat on the hill that rose behind the Dukes family farmhouse, took stock of everything that had happened in the past few weeks, and scanned the news on his phone that the prime minister would be holding a special ceremony to honor all those involved in both fighting the fire and the rescue effort. These men and women in camo pants and red jackets who'd leaped into danger to save their fellow Canadians from disasters big and small were the people that he had chosen to serve alongside. They were his new work family. And the closer he and Quinn grew, the more he found the ambivalence than had overwhelmed him subsiding and his heart igniting with his former passion to serve his country and rescue those in need.

It had been six weeks since Big Poppa had been arrested, running from the flames barely a mile from the cabin he'd set just set alight. And Jeff was oddly thankful that arson had been added to the list of charges Kirk was facing, along with murder, attempted murder and kidnapping. Kelsey had recovered and pleaded guilty, along with her brother Benny. A handful of other criminals who'd helped Kirk with various parts of the scheme had been found and charged as well.

Thankfully, Quinn's business had rebounded like a phoenix, thanks to the idea of her new freelance media consultant Marcel that they presell packages where campers didn't know where they were going until they got there. The concept had taken off like hotcakes with mystery-loving millennials and she'd already sold out over six months in advance. And Jeff had taken the money he'd wanted to give her and used it for a down payment on a house just down the road from her family's. Bit by bit, every stray thread was being tied.

Which just leaves the fears in my heart, Lord, Jeff prayed. *Help me continue to face them, fight them, heal and grow into the man who Addison, Quinn, my friends and my country need me to be.*

"One, two, three, go!" Addison's voice shouted from the trees behind him.

His heart soared as he watched as Quinn and Addison burst through the leaves, holding hands as they ran down the hill together. They reached the ground, tumbled into the grass and rolled, giggling. Then they started back up the hill again. Quinn flashed a dazzling smile at him as they passed.

How he had ever found a woman so amazing to agree to be in his life was beyond a mystery. But ever since they'd been rescued from the rock together, he'd made good on his promise to her and to God to be a better man and stand by her side. He'd met with the therapist his brother had recommended, who, to be honest, hadn't been a good fit, but had a second appointment with another he liked a lot better. He'd also attended a few meetings of the trauma support group and, while he hadn't been ready to open up and talk about what had happened overseas, he found listening to other people's stories and hearing the advice they shared with each other really helped and reminded him he wasn't alone.

His phone buzzed to announce an email had arrived. He opened it and was startled it to see who it was from.

Paul.

"One, two, three!" Addison shouted again.

"Quinn!" Jeff called and stood so he could see them through the trees. "When you're done this trip, can you join me for a second?"

Her eyebrow quirked. "Absolutely."

He watched as they careened through the trees together one more time. Then Quinn took Addison over to the farmhouse porch, where Rose stood flipping burgers, Leia was setting out food, and Butterscotch was having an animated discussion with Moses the cat, who was lazily watching the enthusiastic puppy through the window.

He watched as Quinn turned and walked up the hill toward him. Sunlight fleeced her limbs and seemed to dance in her eyes. His mouth went dry. Then she was by his side, brushing his lips with a kiss and taking his hand in hers. They sat on the ground.

"What's up?" she asked.

"I just got an email back from Paul," he said. "Someone in my trauma group suggested I write to him, so I did, and he replied. But I haven't read it yet. I'm kind of worried about what it might say."

"How about I read it for you?" she asked. She held out her hand and he gave her the phone.

"'Dear Jeff,'" she read. "'Thank you for your kind email and your congratulations on my recent wedding. I have to admit I never expected to hear from you. I'm really sorry for how miserable I made things after Della died. I was hurting a lot, but that doesn't justify my taking it out on you. I appreciate the offer to be part of Addison's life. To be honest, I don't think I'll ever take you up on it. Actually, my lovely wife and I are expecting a child of our own. But if you or Addison ever need anything, feel free to reach out. Paul.'"

He let out a long breath.

She handed him back the phone. "That was kind of him," she said, "and it was good of you to reach out and try to make peace."

"Thanks," he said and looked out over the trees. "I'm beginning to see just how much I misjudged a lot of people, including myself."

She didn't answer for a long time and when he looked back, he was surprised to see she was frowning.

"Is everything okay?" he asked.

"I think so," Quinn said, worry filling her eyes. "You've just seemed really distracted all day and then you needed some time alone to think, and I'm worried if something's wrong with you. Are you okay?"

"Quinn, I am more than okay," he said and reached for her hand. "I am unbelievably happy. You make me the happiest I've ever been."

"You make me happy too," she said. She turned to face him. Their knees bumped. "But, am I right that something's on your mind?"

How did she know him so well? "There is."

"Well, then share it will me and let me help you," she said.

"I can't—"

"Yes, you can—"

"Fine," he said. "I've been sitting here alone, reviewing the events of the past few weeks in my mind, because I've been trying to figure out how to ask the woman I'm in love with to marry me! I even went to the store yesterday and looked at all these traditional gold and diamond engagement rings that didn't look like anything you might want to wear. They all seemed wrong for you."

Her eyes widened and, for a long moment, he just gazed into the face of the woman he knew without a doubt he wanted to spend the rest of his life with. Then she leaned her forehead against his.

"The camping equipment store sells silicon bands for about twenty bucks," she whispered. "They're great because you don't have to take them off while climbing or canoeing. They'll even replace it if it breaks."

He chuckled softly. "I didn't know that."

"Well, you should've asked me," she said with a smile.

"And if a guy bought you one of those silicon rings and asked you to be his wife, would you say yes?" he asked.

She pulled back and looked him in the eyes. "Only if that man was you."

"Good," he said. "Because I'm determined to spend the rest of my life with you."

"Deal." Joy illuminated her eyes. "I'm going to hold you to that."

"Please do," he said. "I love you, Quinn."

"I love you too," she said. "And I want to marry you, raise Addison alongside you, have a family with you, and share all of my life adventures with you for the rest of my life."

"Sounds like a plan," he said.

Then he gathered her into her arms and kissed her deeply, before they stood, linked hands and walked down to the house to tell Addison the good news.

* * * * *

If you enjoyed this story, look for these other books by Maggie K. Black:

Witness Protection Unraveled
Christmas Witness Conspiracy
Undercover Protection

Dear Reader,

As I was working on an early draft of this book, I looked out the window and saw my neighbor trying, and failing, to train his adorably stubborn golden retriever puppy to walk on a leash. Many years ago, when I was in college, I walked my cat in a harness and leash when I lived downtown, and that was a major challenge! The cat absolutely loved being outside but had no interest in "walking," choosing instead to dash madly from spot to spot, occasionally leaping up trees or even onto my shoulder. But walking Tandia the tabby was a breeze compared to what my neighbor was going through as he tried to coax his pup to please stop rolling around on my lawn. Finally, he gave up, picked up the dog and carried him.

I'm thrilled to share that this book will be my twenty-fifth Love Inspired Suspense and I'm incredibly grateful to my editor Emily Rodmell for all of her help, support, hard work and guidance on this journey.

If you're familiar with my stories, you'll know I've written about a lot of brave, noble, well-trained and protective dogs who've defeated evil and saved characters from harm. For this book, I wanted to write about a dog more like my own two beloved small dogs, who sometimes make a mess, knock over the garbage can, refuse to walk, bark at the pizza delivery people, and can be an absolute nuisance. Recently the vet warned me that the fluffy white one is now nearing the end of her life and it has filled me with a fresh appreciation of how much happiness her daily nonsense has brought to my life.

So, here's to all the loveable nuisances in our lives and the joy they bring.

Thank you again to all of you who've shared this journey with me. Your letters and messages fill me with such absolute joy.

Mags

LOVE INSPIRED

Stories to uplift and inspire

Fall in love with Love Inspired—
inspirational and uplifting stories of faith
and hope. Find strength and comfort in
the bonds of friendship and community.
Revel in the warmth of possibility and the
promise of new beginnings.

Sign up for the Love Inspired newsletter
at **LoveInspired.com** to be the first
to find out about upcoming titles,
special promotions and exclusive content.

CONNECT WITH US AT:

 Facebook.com/LoveInspiredBooks

Twitter.com/LoveInspiredBks